# Stubborn

........................................................................

## Chloe Picks

# Contents

# Flash back

1 month back

Prachi pov

Maa Mai ja rhi hu . Dhoop tez ho jayegi. ( Maa I'm going, the sun will be brighter)Her mother (Mrs pritam)Thik hai jao panni lelo.(Okay go , take water)Today sun is very bright. I need to go fast papa is waiting for me .Bike horns :Yes ! Papa I'm here.Her Father (Mr. Diwakar)Jaldi baitho .( Sit fast)I sat on bike . My right eye is twitching don't know what the hell is going to happen!!!Uffff....

Papa please drive fast.

Author pov-

Prachi and her father left for town , her father had some official work and she joined just for shopping stuffs.After reaching she all alone gone to the main market while her father was nearby doing some official work.

Prachi pov-

Bhai saheb itni dhoop m bhi log aa jate h bheed lagane.Wait a sec..... Why is he crying ????? Rikshawpuller ?? Is he hurt? I need to see....Please give me side please!! These people can't help but always ready to make mess out there!I saw a man sitting on the road in between the people,his right hand is on forehead. Oh my god!!!!! He's bleeding!!! I started panicking,my legs started trembling!! This is my phobia in these kinda situation as if I will fall down out of trembling!!!

I saw a medical shop , I cooled myself down and ran towards it and got some cotton , one antiseptic cream and one bandage.It was again a difficult task for me to get inside these many peoples!!

I saw a different view now , people were holding responsible a man with 3-4 police man protecting him! Out of the blue I shot a video in my phone .

Keeping it for a while aside, I took step towards the rikshawpuller.

I got him bandage , by applying cream and then cover it with cotton and then bandage.

The man who was in protection of police came near rikshaw puller and tried to get him up of the road. While being injured he can't even stand. He's very very disgusting!! Don't have humanity, what on Earth is he for?

Author pov-

Rajveer was holding the rikshawpuller hand and trying to making him stand with his full force unknown about his leg got fractured!!

Prachi all of sudden hit a slap on rajveer face . Police standing behind rajveer came front and tried to hold prachis hand for taking her to custody!

She lost all her sence and stated targeting them with her hars words and making them feel guilty what they did and are trying to cover things up. People in support started cherishing her.

Rajveer pov -

I just came to make things done , taking that rikshaw puller to doctor if needed! I held his hand and tried to make him stand although he was not able to but maybe he was in trauma of all these so I forced myself more to make him stand.All of a sudden someone slapped on my cheek!??Whatt?? Why?? Who dare it?? I took my head up I saw a girl will fair skin tone , her face turns red may be for what courage she needed to slap me!!Her hairs were on all over her face ,She wore a red crop top with light blue jeans .Out of the jerk , her top button open and I saw her juicy boobs .

I just wanted to suck it and make my mark all over boobs !!Her voice took me out of that world , she was messing with my protection forces.I recall at of sudden she slapped me while ago. How can she ? I want to slap her back , of course also in punishment I want to fuck her!!!

We will continue! If you are liking the story please let me know by comments! If something is not right I'm sorry for that ! Spices will come now and  will never end  because you can summarise that rajveer is not letting her go and will make her regret!!

# 15 days

-------------------------------------------------------------

A uthor pov

Rajveer is focused on her boobs , and her lips . Phone rings : it's of prachi her father calling her!!!

Prachi pov-

Hello! Haan papa

Mr diwakar-

Kaha ho?aao tower ke pass!!

Prachi - haan bas 1 min whi hu

What the hell is this!! Why was he focusing on my boobs ... Looked down Shitttttt mannnn fuck this button!!For the first time I wore it and isne apni aukaad dikha di!! That's the reason why I always wear short kurti instead of tops !!Oh god!! I'm so embarrassed! He might be thinking I did it knowingly to seduce him! Fuck!!!What kind of man was he ? Wait I have a video that can be used against him to take legal action!He can't use his power!! Either he's politician or an officer. No he might be a politician he was in formal !But officers always don't wear their dress!Let it be! I'll send it the commissioner via email.Oh god again mess, thinking all this I moved far from tower . Comon prachi step back.

Rajveer -

This was literally un imaginable. Thank you God for saving me out there . These people will occupy road as it is of there father and then will play victim! Rascals!!!

Have done bandage over rishkapullar feet and given him medicine prescribed by Dr . I also paid 20000 for that for his fruits and family household as he can't earn for a while!

That girl! Red top..... Her lips her boobs I want to destroy that with my teeth!! What color of her nipples would be? Brown? Pink?black? I don't care I want to tear that aprat. I know I'm a womaniser but I only fuck them and pay them nothing like foreplay or I have to do with upper body parts!!But her!! I want to taste her lips, her boobs, her pu&sy . I want to feel inside her , how does it feel when she will scream my name in pain & pleasure??

Oh fuck!! It's getting hard ! I can't do anything now I'm on duty. I have not even seen her face , leave her (my mind said) I'll give you a treat tonight I said thik to my dick while Patting!!

Authors pov

Prachi reached her house and after getting fresh she send mail to commissioner of area with the videos.Requesting him to take against rajveer!As soon as the commissioner saw the mail and looked into the matter at glance all the clue was against rajveer , he gave the suspension letter to rajveer for 15 days until the whole matter is disclosed. Either he will have clean chit or suspension for entire life.

Rajveer pov

Sir this is not the whole story! You can  ask people on the spot I had bills of him getting his treatment done and the fault is not ours.That man came in between all of sudden with his riskha we were driving safely please sir .

Commissioner pov-

Till the investigation is going on you are suspended that's my final order. I don't need any explanation. Can leave.

Rajveer pov-

Sir don't you know me? I can't do that!

Commissioner pov-

Yes I know you so I don't want you to fall in trap , the raid where you gave made in past are behind you because you didn't took bribe and send them behind bars. Before it reaches to them I need to settle it down.

Author pov-

Rajveer in anger and frustration left the room . After greeting jai hind!!

Another update soon as this is my first story and rajveer is too hungry to satisfy his male ego .

# Mission accomplished

---

Hi guys!! Hope you will enjoy it . Please ignore words wrongly spell. I'm new , don't know how to write and make emphasis that well. Thankyou

Prachi pov - Im satisfied now , if the commissioner doesn't take action against him ill leak it to different pages holding millions followers.

A notification pop up

Who's messaging me now! Mail from commissioner!! Finally he has suspended him huuufff....Thank God .

Rajveer pov

While I was returning from sir's chamber my friend told me that a girl is responsible for my suspension, her name is " PRACHI PRIYADARSHINI ".

I used my official trackers, to know about adress and location, I found she is same girl with jucy boobs.

I'm not going to leave her I decided and send my man to collect information about her.

He brought information she is aged 23 , living with her parents, middle class family , father is principal, Brahman caste, 2 siblings , pursuing masters. Mission accomplished!!!!

Now I'll show you how the hell it feels when someone ruins your self respect without any fault .I have decided I'll marry her make her life hell , I'll crush her self respect her body her ego every single day .

We will meet soon maybe tomorrow!!!

Authors pov -

Rajveer is mad at prachi wanting to take revenge he went to bed room directly, without uttering a single word his mother ( Mrs Rupa) is worried about him. She has entered room without his permission dailed pasword and door opened.

Mrs Rupa pov-What happened beta ? Why are so upset!!

Rajveer- mom I wanted to tell you something!

Rupa- yes tell me beta Im here for you

Rajveer - I'm in love with someone, I know caste and family matters to you she is of our caste .

Rupa - no need to tell that, if she is your happiness I'll do whatever you want.

Rajveer - I want to marry her within a month because I can't live without her.

Rupa - don't worry this will happen, I'll talk to your dad.

Rajveer - thankyou mom.

( Game begins)

Prachi pov -

Resting on my bed I heard my father talking to someone.It's 11pm and we sleep early around 10 pm. I choose to go in papa room and listen the conversation.

When I entered call cuted!! I was late !!Papa kon tha itni raat m?

Papa- tumhare liye ek rishta aaya h bahot aacha h , ham b khoj he rahe the , itni hasiyat to nhi hai ke khud se itni bari Ghar m krte bhagwan ne aage se veja h .

I was shocked heinnn!!!!!???Ladka kya krta h - I asked

Papa - ladka ips officer h , uske papa commissioner hoke retired h , ek bhai ek behan h ladka tumhari tarah.bahot aacha Ghar parivaar h .

Me- to wo mujhse kyun shaadi krna chahte hain? Mujh m kya h?

Papa- ladka ne khi tumhe dekha h syd usse tum bahot psnd ho isliye I was like he wanted marry me , when he saw me .I was all confused.I told my papa to show me his pics .

Papa- they will send it tomorrow!Ohkhy papa.I went to sleep out, lot of mixed up and my headache started.

In morning Rajveer rajveer utho beta ( Mr Pawan )

Rajveer - yes good morning dad.

Pawan- I talked to her father yesterday, your mom gave me the number. They are very happy.

Rajveer sat out of sock!

You talked to her father seriously??

Pawan- yes I did and responce is good.I'll send your pic today.

Rajveer - ohkhay dad.

Let's see now how many days your little pussy is out of my range Mrs rajveer thakur.(Rajveer in his mind)

Author pov-

Mr Pawan has send photos of rajveer to Mr diwakar, he was very impressed, when he saw this to prachi she was very shocked. She remembered his face whose eyes  was one and only on her boobs. His behaviour towards rishkapullar... She instantly said I don't wanna marry him!!! That's it.

Mr diwakar - why? Leave it if you are so sure about it I won't force.ill tell them you are not interested.

Prachi - I just want to , thankyou for understanding me papa. (Hug)

Rajveer pov -

Let's see what that girl do to my proposal!

Door opens Mr Pawan came inside.

Mr Pawan - she rejected your proposal her father said she's not interested!!

Rajveer brusted in anger - okay dad .

Went to bathroom locked the door.

Rajveer pov-How dare she ! She is playing with fire I need to teach her lesson right now today . I won't leave her ,I will make sure and I'm promise myself that today is 29th March before 29th April she will be with me in this shower.

Author pov-

For an hour rajveer took bath to cool down his temper. His father still waiting outside and worried about him he knows rajveer can do anything to make his wish ful full. He's very passionate about what he wants.

Prachi pov-

What the hell! How can he search me ! I'm not afraid of him . I'll show him what I made up of.i know you are after me but you will never get me.

I need to go to temple for prayers so that this monster leaves me. Forget about me . I need my heart and mind to feel peace .

Maa where is papa?Mrs Pritam - today's his meeting he will be going now.Prachi- I will catch me just a min

I dressed myself in short white kurti and flared baggy jeans. Thinking of what has happened the day before.

I left with papa and in half of the I told him to drop me.I'm in auto now ! Main town is 20-30km far from my home.

It's very good to see people with different attitude around me.

I'm listening songs, dekhe kismai kitna hai dam!!!

I reached the main market.Temple is almost 5-10min away from it.

Again why the fuck this eye start twinkling!! I'm an empath and usually get instincts if something right or wrong is about to happen!!!

Rajveer pov-

She is 2 min away!!

His driver- sir right or left?

Rajveer - right 70m away from us . Stop the car now.

Author pov- Rajveer has been tracking prachi from yesterday, from when he got to she was behind his suspension. Un aware of it she is roaming freely. She gets into the temple and offers prayers, while steping out of the temple she got a call.

Another chapter is going to be  if I make you wait I'm sorry for that. I will continue it .

If you like please let me know things will spice

# Her taste (+18)

P rachi -Haan papaMr diwakar - outside the boundary of the temple a black Mercedes is waiting for you.

Prachi- who's waiting inside??

Mr diwakar - he's the same boy who wanted to marry you . He wants to meet you know the reason why you don't want to marry him!

Prachi- papa what are you telling! You are sending me with a man to whom either I don't know nor you!! What's wrong with you???!!!

Mr diwakar - he was begging baccha , his father told me that he was very upset I'll in touch he send me his live location don't worry!! He and his family are gentleman.

Prachi - I'll not go at any cost papa bye I'll take an auto now.

Mr diwakar - who is telling you to go with him just meet him I'll on call , I request you afterwards what will be your decision Ill respect that

Prachi - will see

Mr diwakar - let me know weather you meet him or not in an hour.

Prachi - okay bye papa

Rajveer pov -

Come fast butterfly I want to taste you !! It's either do or die . You will have to marry me at any cost.

Author pov-

Prachi with her heavy steps moved forward just two steps and saw a black Mercedes she was dead inside. She don't know what will happen. Meanwhile, Mr diwakar forced her because he knows her daughter she is very innocent and have pure heart she needs a decent men to look after her and he finds rajveer and his family perfect for her, he searched for their life and position in society everything was very well and good . So he wanted to marry him and have a dreamy good life.

Prachi pov-

I'm sweating! I knocked the door !! Door automatically opened. I saw him on the other side looking at me . My heart beatfaster . He said to get me inside. With lots of fear  I get into the car. Door closed. He was still staring at me.I am feeling uncomfortable as hell.

Rajveer - so why don't you want to marry me prachi?

Prachi- likewise I don't think we will be ideal couple !

Rajveer- who wants to be an ideal couple! I'll show you what I want to be !!Shield the glasses! (I ordered a driver)All the glasses turned black after my order, I opened the curtains which were between the driver and the back seat , and on the windows of the car.

I tied it and told my driver to increase the song volume. Now I'll show her what am I!!!

Prachi pov- Why are you doing all this? What the hell are you doing. I smell danger.

All of sudden he holded my hands up of my head and by a push he laid me into his back seat. It was that fast I was unable to process what is happening!!!

I'm very much scared I want to cry no one can help me god please save me please please.

He has came on the top of me . I brusted into tears I can't hold it now.

Rajveer pov-I know she has senced something I don't want to give her time to process it. I holded her hand and I'm top of her now. She is crying like a baby. Her faces has turned red. Which make my dick hard and wanted to just fuck her roughly and make her cry into scream.

The way she is resisting proves that she is virgin!!! I will break her virginity!! I want to break it now. But I'm controlling myself she can't take me.

Authors pov-

Rajveer has started kissing passionately to Prachi. Bitting her lips to get entrance inside her mouth. But she closed it very hard with teeth.

Rajveer pov-

She thinks she can escape! poor she!I holded her hands with my left hand while my right hand stated moving down. I lifed her top.... Her juicy boobs were cased in her tight bra.

Shut your mouth and be like an ideal girl or I'll fuck you that hard you won't be able to go home. I yelled at her.

Unbelievable she stopped, resisting it, looking like a cute rabbit who is scared of lion.Tears were just rolling out of her eyes.I drank all that.I lifted her slightly up and opened her bra button.She closed her eyes with force.My toung are dying to take that inside it and suck it.I had chocolate inside my seat I leaned and got one dairy milk silk. I took a bite crumbed it and spell it all over her boobs I kept it aside for her pu$sy.

She was trembling in fear. I bite on her lower lip and sucked it for a min and came down . I sucked her neck and bite it again sucked it .now her boobs were going up and down which look like heaven.

I left a mark over her neck left side and shifted my head towards her juicy and naughty boobs.I licked of the choclate first she is breathing heavily. Now its time to give her punishment.

I took left bud inside mouth suked it for 5 mins and then I stated chewing and bitting it. She is in pain and pleasure. I increase my sucking and bitting, there was mark all over her left boob .  I wanted to stop but couldn't help . I downed my head again and look right bud in grap when I sucked it she stated bitting her lower lip and head rolled backwards. I got a sign she is in control now. I stated sucking it hard

Ahhhh.... Please don't bite it please it hurts please ( prachi said)

All words were blured I just heard her moan.

I stated opening her jeans button she was shocked!!

No Don't I can't tolerate this much please I bited on her nipples Ouch ahhh.... I kept biting just to take her attention that way.

I opened her button and now her womanhood is going to be nacked.I slip down my right hand in her panty she came into sence and moved her hips to resist my hand unfortunately it gave me access to her clit.

Poor butterfly!!!I started moving her clit in anti clock wise slowly slowly .Remove your hand you idiot! I'll not leave you I said leave me , leaveee meeee ( she screamed)

I don't want to do my finger ,wanted to break her virginity with my dick , wanted to do now but knowing that she can't handle it all of her first time I step back.

I stated rubbing her pussy fast and faster .

Prachi moaned - rajveerrr ahhhh ahhhh ahhhhh don't please ahhhh my god ahhhhh please don't ahhhhh

I got a grip , opened her jeans full and now panty I split her leg . She somehow manages to lock her thighs , her thighs are thick like many man wants. I want to see her pussy and taste her.

I can't control now I stated rubbing more faster and pinching her clit she moaned again

Rajjj ahhhhahhhh verr ,ahah what are ahhhhhhhhh youuuu DD ahhhhh doinahhhhh doinggggShe spilted it and took a chance and lean down she was about to cum I stopped and leave her pussy all alone .

I don't want her to cum now. I want her to moan my name more . She is breathing heavily biting her lips and opening and locking her leg one after another. After a min I splited her legs again and placed my toung inside her pussy she raised her hip out of pleasure I started licking it I want to be rough. I started doing it fast she was moaning mess . Ahhhh veerr ahhhhhh gooooddddd aahhhh ouch ahhh ahhh .

I bited on it . Harshly

Prachi- ahhhhhhh , she brusted into tears. Don't

I started sucking it again..Ahhhhhh hhhh ahahh ahh ah ah ah ah

I bit it again, and then stretched it with my teeth and then bit it again this .this continues for 10mins .

Prachi- don't do this ahhhhhh ouch ahhhh ahhhhhhhhhahhhhhhhh ahhh ahh ahhh ahhh ahh ahh ah ha ha ahhhh ah ah ah ah ha ahhhh ahhh ah ah ahhhh ah ah ahahhh.rajjjjj ahhh ahhhhhhhhhhh please ahhhhhh ahhh ahhhh ah

She is about to cum she holded my hair tried to remove my face from her pussy. Instead I stated it faster she cummed into my mouth . She tasted like heaven . I gave a bite on vagina and started licking her liquid. She is rolling her hips round up and down. To get settled.

# Pain in her eyes (+18)

R ajveer pov-Even though I have neither inserted my finger nor my dick she is feeling something, I can't conclude either it's pleasure or pain!!!

I was staring at her boobs how it bounces when she breathes up and down. Chocolate took my attention!

I left it for her pussy while applying it on her boobs . I want to lick it .

I held her hand again and locked it on the top of her head.She was nacked all just that the bra was hanging on her neck.

She gazed at me . I took a bite of chocolate and started kissing her roughly.

Prachi pov-

He's biting on my lips it's hurting me!! I never ever thought this type of harassment will happen to me. I can't move my hand , my body it's so painful. I'm naked before a stranger I am on my death bed it seems , I want to die out of embarrassment!!!

How can this happen to me??? How ?? Did I do that bad?? Is my karma that worst ?? That I deserve this??? I'm dead I don't know how will I face myself in mirror!!!

He's trying hard to get his toung inside my mouth I can't let him he is a rascal .

I want to run and disappear!why it's hurting down in my pussy!?

Oh nooo!! Again!! He rubbed it licked it and bite it leaving me in pain . At certain points it was pleasure but was not of my concent I consider it a pain.

Ahhhhh please stop your hand ummmm ahhhh ahh ahhh ahhhh stoo ahhhhh don't ahhh please ahhhh ahh .

He suddenly started streching my clit rubbing it and pinching it, my pussy is very hurted he bited it before I'm feeling like burn.

When I scream he inserted his toung my mouth .

Rajveer pov -

She don't know who am I !! Huhh I know every tactics to make a girl open her ass , pussy, mouth , clothes everything!!

I kissed her roughly very roughly bited on her toung , inner lips , lips so that she remember me till our wedding!!

Tears is rolling out of her eyes.I don't want to look at her, she do something to me I calm down!! I don't wanna forget what she has done to me !! I'm suspended for 15 days and she is living happily is not fair!!

I told her leaving her lips and tongue if you dare to resist and make any kinda indecent thing I'll fuck you right now and you know I can!!

She just nodded keeping her hand on her lips.

I slided down and took one bite of dairy milk and spread with my tongue to her inner thighs and on her pussy she screamed out of pain .

I have roughly licked it few minutes ago , but I want to lick that again I want to listen her moan and making her feel pain how does it look like when someone is targeting your dignity without any fault!!!

I started licking it , she is holding seat of the car tightly to resist herself.I am careful now I can't bite it or rub it she can't hold it more!!!I am just licking her pussy softly I eat all chocolate on it and lastly I just wanted to give one long love bite on her clit and top of the vagina.

I choose clit first .I started sucking it she can't hold it she is pulling my hair and scratching my shoulder so that I leave her!!

No baby !! Not now I depth my mouth more into it and started sucking it roughly she again brusted into tears, I bite it and left !! She was literally in pain!! She is biting car seat out of pain.

I can't see it anymore. I holded her head and made her sit.

She screamed maaa and crying like hell .What the fuck I done to her! I should be careful! I don't know but drop of tears came out of my eyes after seeing her in extreme pain.

I was very rough to her even experienced get pain in this much harness she is just virgin and its her first touch!!

Fuck!!! I'm a duffer!!!I holded her shoulder and hugged her while massaging her hair. She is beating on my shoulder . I understand her frustration! I tighten my grip .

After a min she is relaxed now . I got tissues thought to clean her ! But I don't have that guts to do that after seeing her in that condition.

We aprated!!She doesn't looked at me and started wearing her clothes.I holded her hand , she was trembling like what will I do now!!I said so what's your decision now ?

Prachi- ......

Rajveer - I asked something! Are you deaf! ( I'm trying to take over my heart for staying focused on what I want her to marry me)

Prachi- ....

Rajeev - (higher his pitch) don't you dare to test my patience prachi !! I asked something what is your decision on marrying me??

Prachi - my- decision-! It's -your- decision- to- marry- me ,( voice shaking into pieces)

Rajveer - yes it's my decision and I want you to marry me .

Prachi- If I don't!!

Rajveer - you better know the consequences this was trailer! And on second thought your father can be trapped by officers in illegal and fraud activities!!

Prachi- what? How dare you to invlove my family into this!!

Rajveer - I can involve your whole generation, upcoming generation into it . Want to see demo!!

Prachi- feeling helpless she said - yes I'll marry you. With havey heart!!

Author pov- after that prachi requested driver to stop the car but he hasn't as rajveer didn't gave permission, after a second car stopped she was outside her gate. She get down of the car but couldn't walk properly as she pussy was harrased by rajveer she was feeling pain down there.She was to fell down but took wall as a support and gone inside her main gate didn't looked back.Seeing this rajveer said don't worry I teach you each and every thing .

# can't be helped (+18)

-----------------------------------------------------------

Prachi pov-I needed to take a bath.

Mrs pritam- why are you crying? Kya hua beta ko?!! Thik ho Babu ?!!( She hugged her)

Prachi - ( I can't hide it now all the pain came out of my eyes)kuch nhi maa , sar dard kr rha h !!

Mrs pritam- nhi juth!! Kya usne kuch Kiya h? Ye lip Kate Kate se kyun hain tumhare??!!

Prachi- maa please kya krega koi mere sath, bahar bahot tez dhoop h iss wajah se kat gye honge !

Mrs pritam- thik h , take shower I'll make tea for you.

Prachi pov-

I nodded and went towards bathroom. I opened shower when water touched my body it feels like someone is touching my skin with hot iron . It is irresistible pain !! On my boobs and my vagina. I turned off the shower. I started wearing my clothes without using towel.

Maa was ready with the tea. I took it and sat with her.She said that in marriage there is lots of sacrifices and compromises every couple has to do .I gave a smirk to myself thinking all this is one and only for me not for him.I talked with her for half an hour and told her that I'll be sleeping now so don't disturb me or worry about me.

Maa- okay take rest . I'll wake you up at evening.

Me- hmm and went to my room locked my door.

Their was no mirror in bathroom,I started un clothing my self to look what he has done to my body.

He ate my breasts , my lips my vagina there were biting marks all over my body especially these parts.

I never looked myself naked in mirror, Today it's first time and I'm ashamed of my self I can't see my face in it . He made me do that I hate him I really hate him.

I don't know what to do , I just bend my head to knees and slept on floor I don't want to go on my bed , Im feeling very hurted , my soul is crying as if someone raped my soul.

After 2 hours....Hey kesav hey madav hey govind...... My phone rings , I was awaken by it.

It's an unknown number

Hello.. who's this?!!

Other side- this is your would be husband my butterfly!!

Me - rajveer?

Him- yes ! How are you feeling now does it hurt till now?

I am mad at him . I wanted to kill him.

I cuted the call . And muted my phone . He stated calling in on WhatsApp I muted him everywhere.I couldn't block him , he will create a mess again.

Somebody knocked on the door.I stood up and wore my clothes I slept naked .After wearing I opened it .Papa when you came?Papa-Just now!!Come let's go for snacks

Me- yes he congratulated me and took me for evening snacks..

After 1 week...

Authors pov-

Prachi is living a peaceful life by muting him from everywhere. Their marriage is fixed on 15April . She doesn't want to do any pre wedding functions.

Her exams are coming before her wedding she wake up by 3 am and study afterwards. Because of weeding there is crowd only a week is left.

Rajveer pov-

She has became very daring now a days I need to teach her lesson again.Her father told to dad about her routine she woke up early ...(Devil simle) Let's meet today Mrs prachi rajveer thakur.

I am waiting for night, I made plan to enter her house .

I need to sleep now . I have lots of work to do one of them is punishing my butterfly so that she can't even think of ignoring me.

Its almost 1am . My alarm rang. My house is almost 100 km away from her. So we booked a hotel for weeding functions.

And her house is 30 km away from here.I'm all set it's 1:45 . I'm out in my car.I'll reach there at almost 3 am.

Prachi pov-

(Alarm rang of 2:45 ) I turned it off and fresh myself and came for studies. I'm not traumatized girl , I'm very preculiar about my body , I can't tolerate if someone touches it in either ways .

I had been this because of some past events!!!

I don't know why my heart is beating fast!!

Rajveer pov-

I stopped the car at 100m away from her house.I don't wanna trouble her!!I started jogging from there and reached her house in 2 min .From today it's almost 3 am so , I'll be joining the duty again there was nothing against me and I got I rejoining letter.One more reason to taste her water I want to celebrate it by making her moan.

There is boundary in her house I need to climb it and get into the house.

Door is opened because my father in law goes for walking at 4 am he use to open it early.

I saw 2 rooms with an opened light . Murmuring sound was coming from one room. Ohh mann this is my in laws talking!!I stepped forward in second room I saw her studying on bed .She has wore black jogger and white tshirt.

I entered into room without making any noise.

Prachi pov-

My door opened...... What the heck how can he !! He entered into my room god !! Fuck !! No way!!! My heart is beating fast it will blast now.

Rajveer pov-

She is reading something on her phone. I entered and locked the room.I grabbed her phone . She got trauma . After seeing me

I checked her phone my number is not even saved in her phone. Their is 1500+ messages on WhatsApp 500+ calls . She dare to mute me.

Wait butterfly!!! I holded her hand she was about to escape from the room.

I pushed her on the bed and locked her hand up to her head.

She is again trying to resist!!!

Prachi - leave me ! How dare you to come into my room. Just go from here!!

Rajveer - I dare to do many things who wants me to do that ??

Prachi- I will call papa right now he will see what kinda person you are and will call off weeding I'll show you who I am ,leave me you pervert!!

Rajveer - call him! If you want that your whole collony should know I entered your room call him. Your father's respect will be ruined.

Prachi - what do you want now!you have done what you wanted , Leave me please .

Rajveer - I want you to shut the fuck up and open your bra and sit on my lap .

Prachi - are you mad or what?? You think I ll do that. ??

Rajveer - if I started doing it out first night will be celebrated before our marriage, you want that?

Prachi- why are you doing this please!!

Rajveer - I'll count upto 5 afterwards you are responsible.

Prachi - leave my hand first .

Rajveer - you are free now countdown starts - 1..... 2.....3......4.... Fa.

She suddenly sat on my lap.I tried to kiss her She held my head and started resisting.

I told her to open her bra and tshirt..I started to open it , he held my hand and stopped me.

She opened her bra herself was looking very beautiful without it . Her tears were coming to her nipples she looks very sudective . She sat on my lap , I took her leg parted that and placed it on both sides of my waist.

I was just wondering how can a girl be so obedient?? She follows my every instruction in that. Keeping it on other side.

I started sucking her boobs. She moaned ahhhh ,.... She freed her hand from my grip I locked it with my hand on her waist before.

Not now I'm in mood!! She started resisting.... I holded her hair took my face close to her and said. Your hole is on target if you do it again I'll not care it's your first time I'll insert my whole length inside you.

If you don't want it stop this right now. She usually cried and stopped it. I took her both hand and kept it on my shoulder. She has closed her eyes, her neck and boobs are coated with her tears.

Started licking it , she is fasting her breath. I took her left nipple inside my mouth and I started sucking it she is scratching my back , I'm feeling horny !! Rajveer please (her), I bite on her nipples Prachi- ouch don't please Rajveer - sucking,

Prachi- please maa and papa are there

Rajveer - bited it again this time hardly

Prachi-- ahhhhh ahhh ahhh don't sorry ahhhh

Rajveer -My dick is hard now , to satisfy it I hold her waist and started rubbing it on my dick . I don't want to lose my control!!But there was pant my little couldn't feel her pussy.

Rajveer - sucking and biting  Prachi- please be gentle ouch ahhhhh ouch ouch be slow ouch ouch ouch ahhhh ahhhh ahhhh

I bited she holded my hairs I gave a mark. I want to remove her jogger But after sucking. I took her in and layed her on floor in a bridal style.

She is not uttering a word. I saw her and then started sucking her boob and massaging her left boob.

I bite it again she moaned ahhhhhh I increased my Speed, biting and sucking her boobs and slaping it She is moaning ahhhhh ahh ahhhhhh ahhh ahhhhhhhhhhhhhhhhh I bite it and left.Be gentle please it hurts ahhhhh ouch !

I took her belly button on charge now I'm licking it and thrusting my toung inside it.

Ahhhh rrr ahhhhh my ahhhh ahh ahhhhhh ahhhhhhh ahhhhhhhhhhhh

She started moving her hips I got her point that's her belly button.

To satisfy her I slided down and opened her jogger she was in panty I started licking it .

She is wet ,. finally!! On the first lick I got it. I wanted to trusted her pussy with toung , I opened her panty she was all wet . I started licking it sucking it .

Ahhh ahhhhhhhhhhhhhhhhh don't ahhhhh ahhhhh ahhh ahh ah ahhhhhh ah ah ah yes ahhhhh ahhh ahhhhhhh fuck ahh ahhhh ahhhhhh ah ah ah

She is moaning like mess. I parted her pussy with my left hand and twisted my tongue inside it ahhhhhhh goddddd ahhhhhhhhh hahaha ahhhhhh .

I started rubbing her clit roughly Prachi - ahhh ouchhh ahhhhhh ahhhhha hhhhhhhh pl ahhhhh Raj ahhhhh ouch ouch ouch ahhhh ahh ahh

She is enjoying the punishment!!!I increase my trust.

Ahh hahhh ah ah ahhhhh ahahhaa ah veer ahhh ahhh ahhh Lea ahhhh-hhhhh ah ah ah ah I am not letting her to complete her sentence .

She was about to cum I came out of her pussy. I opened my pant my dick wanted to taste her cum.

It wanted to bathe in !! It was already harden veins were popping up .She looked at it and got scared, she was moving backwards, I will not let that happen, I holded her thighs parted her legs , she is worried about seeing my dick length , her lips and legs are trembling!! Passed my both hand between her legs and holded her hand this made spread her legs . Again I freed her one hand and hold her both hand with my left hand .

Prachi- please what are you doing!!! I'll die please don't do this please!!!

I am not fucking you idiot . Shut your lip . She closed her eyes with fear.

I took my dick and started rubbing it on her clit and vagina. Seriously,she will be in pain whenever I fuck her. It's big can't be fitted in her little pussy easily.

I increase my rubbing speedShe is moaning- ohhh ahhhh ahahaha leave aahhaha what are ahhhh ah ahhhh doing ahhhh ahhhhh ... In a min she cum. I dick was bathed in it , my dick wanted to fuck her badly but can't.

I don't want to fuck her before marriage and this room is not sufficient for that , I know she will scream like hell and I don't want it to be heard by anyone. I just wanted to listen her moaning and screaming when I fuck her without any inruption and fear.I want to see her crying while taking me inside her and then bouncing her hip in pleasure!!!

# warning (+18)

-------------------------------------------------------

P rachi pov-

I don't want to lie , it was heaven when he was rubbing his dick over my pussy!! I felt like I was on clouds, his balls were trying to thrust themselves in my hole it was so much pleasure, I forgot that rascal was forcing himself on me .I was feeling sweet pain on my upper vagina he bit it roughly. My eyes were closed and I was enjoying it . This was my first time when my little was under a hard rod.

I cumed on his dick! It felt so fulfilling. He started licking it, my poor pussy!!His dick was big and healthy venis were trying to tear that apart and come out of it . I saw it before he took his cock on my pussy.

Im really scared of his dick it will snap off my Little.

He's still licking my liquid I'm trying to control my moan.

This man made me mad.

Ahhhhhhhhh verrr ahhhhhhhhhhhhhhhhhhhhhhhhhhhhhhhhhhhhhhhh don't ahhhhhhhhhhh ahhhhhh ahhhhh ah ah ah.Please don't do this I'm sorry ,

I'll not ignore you again- I said He has sucked my vagina and started biting it again. It is very painful now due to cuts ,he eat it before.

Rajveer pov -

Her pussy has swallown and is red like tomato.I gave her punishment, I want to suck it more but when I touch it she screams i brutally tourched her pussy. It is all cut I can see it. She has still closed her eyes, open your eyes or else I'll bite it again - i said

Prachi pov-I was mad that thought he can take me to heaven, the person who himself belongs to hell how can he take me to heaven.It paining down there. Why ??? Why me always?? He's a womaniser, he is a pervert, a monster how can I Marry him???

He does these things before marriage what will he do after that???;! Im not his sex slave , from next I'll not fear and he will get his answer in my way!!Rajveer threatening me he will bite my cunt again!!!I slowly open my eyes. For I first time I saw him with this much closer .

His eyes !!! His eyes are so beautiful.He has grey pupils and hair is scattered on his forehead. Looking fucking hot.But it can't change my mind to hate him.

He is staring at me !!! A prostitute should be his wife so he can fuck her whenever he wants and she won't complain.

Rajveer pov-

She is looking at me with stillness!! Is she admiring me?!

If you won't reply to my messages or pick my call , I will come on the same day and insert my whole dick inside you and fuck you till you lose your consciousness!!! You get it !! I yelled at her while taking both boobs in my both hands and squeezing it.

Ahhhhh .. she moaned and nodded her head in yes.

I stood up and made her stand too!! She has parted her legs , while standing it's hurting her!! I first made her dressed forcefully. she wanted to do herself in half and hour I don't have time.

I weared my clothes and gave her a forehead kiss tapped on her cheeks with my hand and told her to remember what I said. I left I room.When same way I came inside the house it was almost 5 am. Doesn't matter it's worthy , I tasted her make her moan my name , took her to 7 sky that's all worthy.

I have to leave for my duty at 9 am.I need to drive fast.

Prachi pov -

I can't walk properly!!! I feel like fainted!! He always does the same! I hate him I can't even protect myself !! I can't run from him he'll find me .

I want to die ! Is this the marriage? For what Im marrying him ? Being his sex Toy?? He comes and he harasses me He calls me and harasses me , every single time I met him he has molested me..What he will do after marriage!?? Please god save me !! Please please please I beg you I can't live with him he's a monster.He thinks I'm his food he bite me , chew me, eat me ,suck me .... Why????? Whyyyyyy?? Whyyyyyy?

Authors pov-Prachi burst into tears , it's common that when he suckles and she loses control she gets aroused, but she doesn't want him to force her , he gives her anxiety whenever mate.She doesn't want to marry him but also knows can't run from him. Rajveer is back to his work.Prachi injury is getting hleaded , rajveer calls her random , but doesn't talk something indecent knowing she is always surrounded by her family members.Prachi has focused on her studies.

Only 3 days left for marriage...

Mrs pritam- Beta hmlog mehndi aur Sangeet rakhenge!! Kal

Prachi- nahi maa mujhe nhi rakhna h shaadi se ek din phle Mera exam h please!!

Mrs babita(her paternal aunt) - To padhne se kon mana kar raha hai enjoy kro fir padho shaadi baar baar nhi hoti h!!!

Prachi- bua exams bhi baar baar nhi hoti hai!

Mrs babita - isko to kuch bolna he paglpan h , mat rakho!!

Prachi pov- I went to my room and shut my door I don't want to cry at least today , these people are anxiety in my life , this is not a marriage this is my last right who celebrates it??Papa came to my room

Papa- kya hua beta mehndi nhi krna h?

Me- nahi na papa please meri padhai bhi Puri nhi hue h!!

Uncle ( Mr Daya) - thik hai koi baat nhi dhayan se padho gate laga lo andar se!

Papa- koi jabardasti nhi hai time PE kha pi Lena fir room laga ke padhna taki koi disturb na kre!!

Im feeling blessed I got these supporting mens in my life.

My younger brother is also same as my father

Me - thank you (with a little smile.)

Rajveer pov- Mom mom where are you!! There is crowd. Where will I find her. Mom

Mr Pawan - what happened?

Rajveer - dad my holiday is not granted!! Because I already took it for 10 days from 15 April to 25th April.

Mr Pawan - what?? How will the ceremony will be performed?

Rajveer - I don't know dad!! At least it can be when I come home .

Mr Pawan - yes! That is good idea diwakar ji was telling that bahu don't want to perform any haldi or mehndi .

Rajveer - why? ( I know her she didn't want to because she is marrying me)

Mr Pawan - because of her exams on 14 and marriage is on 15 she will be disturbed!!

Rajveer - okay no issues dad.( I stepped forward)

Mr Pawan - wait veer! I thought to invite her and families to celebrate it together after she gives her exam on 14?

Rajveer - that's good !!! She won't be disturbed and she won't have any of the excuses ( so pre wedding foreplay?)

Mr Pawan - okay I'll inform diwakar ji.

Rajveer - yes dad.

# My would be wife (+18)

-----------------------------------------------

C all rings.....Prachi - yes!

Rajveer - just to remind you that you are coming to my place on the 14th.

Prachi- please! Don't give me taruma now I won't be able to concentrate on my studies!!!!

Rajveer - no butterfly! This decision was taken by our parents I can't help you out.

Prachi- I won't come mark my words!!!

I cut the call!!! He is such a disgusting person he knowingly does that.I don't care I won't go!!!

It's 10 pm already. I should go for dinner!!!

At the dining table....

Mr diwakar - after your exams we will go to celebrate mehndi at damad ji destination.

Prachi - papa please! Don't force me for every single thing out in this world please. I don't want to go and I'll not.

Mr diwakar - I'm not forcing you ,but they have called us and it's a matter of respect try to understand

Mrs pritam- we will in an hour or two

Prachi- please papa please it's very uncomfortable I haven't met them yet all of a sudden I will go and start celebrating with them???

Mrs babita - this girl has a problem from everything, why don't you tell yourself to your father in law? You are so stubborn and selfish....

Prachi- bua ji , I'm selfish leave it !!

Authors pov- Prachi left the dining table out of anger, Mrs pritam followed her and made her understand if she won't go , Mr diwakar will face disrespect and Mr Pawan has announced she will be there tomorrow... She wants both of them to be humiliated? Prachi understood it and said she will visit.On the other side ! The Rajveer family is so excited about their daughter in law, they are planning different things in a unique way. Meanwhile rajveer is making his own plan to taste her again. Prachi knows he won't Leave her tomorrow he will try his best to molest her. With all these feelings all went to their beds.

Next morning....

Mr diwakar - are you ready prachi? It's already 8 am!!!

Prachi - I'm just doing my breakfast papa . 2 mins. I know he will try on me again I'm fully prepared. Please god ,If anyhow today passes he can't touch me for 4 days, ( this is a ritual in Brahmin) I'll see him on the 4th day what to do.

Rajveer - I can't concentrate at my work, I'm waiting for her, my dick is hardened thinking of her just 4 days and she will be mine with the whole of her body.

In the evening......

Prachi pov- My exams were all good , papa and I are going to the hotel , my family members are already there. I hope that man won't join us now . We reached there. They have made very beautiful decorations.

We have our haldi on the 4th day of marriage this is our ritual. The theme of mehndi and Sangeet was pretty and contrasted in yellow and pink.

Mr pawan- please please diwakar ji we all were waiting for you and our bahu Rani.

Mr diwakar - haha!! (Shake hands and hug each other)

Prachi - I touched his feet , he blessed me and told someone to take me to my room to get ready. He told me after that I'll be meeting everyone it's getting late.I needed to take a shower I am so exhausted . She took me to the room , 2 women were there for me . I told them to go and wait for 10-15 min after taking a bath I'll call them.They went outside the room.

I didn't bring any extra pieces of clothes so started opening all of that including my under garments.

I went to the bathroom and opened the shower, I heard someone unlocking the door ,but I have locked it !!! It's all in my head it's just delusional.

Suddenly someone grabs my waist from back! Who's this??? Leave me!!!

Rajveer pov- No one dares to touch my butterfly except me.

Prachi- I am shocked how he came ??? I locked the room !! I'm naked yukkkkk!!!! What the hell !! I'm feeling shy!!

Rajveer - I know what you think I have duplicate keys!! Today she made herself naked !! Her asses are so tempting I won't let her go today!!

I took my hand on her boobs and started massaging it, she is trying to remove it but how can she!??? I smirk!!I took my face to her shoulder and said in her ears don't do it today otherwise you better know!!She has slowed down her resistance.I started squeezing her boobs passionately Ahhhhhhhhh ... She moaned.My dick is getting harder I freed it from the boxer and placed it in  between of her ass cheeks She suddenly stepped on my feet to loose my grip.Are you okay?? I told her !! I'm an ips and you think your basic tactics will work on me?? I laughed!!!But but but you will get punishment for this dare.

I turned her to my face and placed her on the glass wall of the bathroom.

I took my dick and placed it in between her thighs and then spilled her vagina and placed it in between that , my left hand locked her both hand behind her waist and my right hand was playing with her boobs. I like her moaning.I started moving my waist and dick was rubbing on her clit. I took her nipples in my mouth and started sucking it and increased the speed of my waist so that my dick could taste her cum .Ahhhhh ahhhhhhhh ahahahahhahahahah ahhhhhh ahhhhahhhh ahhhhhh ahhhhhha ahahah ah ah ah ahhhhhhhhhhhhhhhh ahh veer ahhhhhhhhh Hhhhhh ahhhhh ahhhhhh ah she's moaning mess.

I took her upper lip in my mouth and increased the speed of my waist more she is in pleasure,on clouds

Ahhhh ahhhh ahhhh ahhhhhh ummmmmmmm ahhhhhhhha ah ahahahah-haha ahhh ahhha ahhhh .She is about to cum. I removed my dick . My dick wanted to tear her pussy apart, and wanted to fill her . I hold my dick again placed inside her thighs.

Veer please, please please at least leave me today please - prachi

Butterfly you are moaning now , not screaming  in pain, your pussy loves my dick .let her play - rajveerNow I held my dick with my right hand and started rubbing it on her clit and hole.Ahhhhh myyyy ahhhhhhh ahh ahhhhhhh mhhhhhhhh ahhhhhhh mmmmmmmm ahhhhhhhh ahahhhhhhhhhh ahhhh ahhhh ahhhh ahhh ahahhahahahah ahhhh ahhhhh ahhhhha hhhhhh ahhhhhh ahhhhha hhhhh ahhhhhh ahhhhhh mmmmmmm fuck me rajveerrr fuckkkkkkk meeeeeee rajjjjjjj ahhhhhhhhhhhh ahhhhh mmmmm

She said to fuck her!???? Oh my god !????? I'm in the air seriously she said me to fuck her!!!!I wanted to but  she wouldn't be able to walk.I want to satisfy her !!! Shitttt if she moaned like this on that day I would fuck her!!

I removed my dick and started rubbing her clit with my fingers!!

Ahhhhh ahhhh yessssss ahhhhhh ahhhhhhhh ahhhhhh rajjjjjjj get ahhhhhh ahhhhhha hhhhhh inside ahhhhh ahhhhhhh ahhhhhhh ahhhhh meeeeee ahhhhhhhh fuckkkkk ahhhhhhhhh mmmmmmm ahhhhhhhh meeeeeee ahhhhhhhhhhhhhhhhhh.- she moaned

I slipped my one finger inside her hole. Ahhhhhhhhhhhh - she moaned

I started moving it slowly she is rolling her hips round up and down I increased my Speed.

Ahhhhhh- ahhhhhh - rajjjjj-ahhhhhhhh ajhhhh ahhhha hahhhhahah ahhhhhh ahhhhha hhhhhhhhhhhhh you ahhhhhhh hahhh yesssss yesssss ahhhhhhh takes me to heaven ahhhhhhhhhhhhhhhhhhhhhhh ahhhhh ahhhh she cummed on my hand.

I held her waist tightly, so that she wouldn't fall down.For the first time she rested her head on my chest!! I felt something different, very relaxing,very calming, I wanted her to rest as long as she wanted to. Her hot breathing is making goosebumps. I kissed her forehead and asked if she was okay.H mmm - she replied I can't leave her  , she is very tired.I took her to shower and made her wash her body.And then held her in bridal style and took her to room, made her sit on bed she stood up like current passed through her body.She started crying!! What happened to her!??? I held her cheeks and asked her what was wrong!?

It's hurting me!! - prachi What ? Down there?? - rajveer Yes!! What have you done to me!!! - prachi

Rajveer - I hugged her and tried to make her calm , butterfly it's your first time you haven't masturbated till date.  What can you expect sweetheart! ??It will be okay don't worry!!

Prachi- who told you that??! Why did you insert your finger??! You are so into sex .

Rajveer - you were moaning haven't you remember few minutes before fuck me rajj fuck me fuck me yes yes!!

Prachi- I didn't remember stop lying.

Rajveer - want to see it again? Think if  your demand was fulfilled and I fucked you with dick ? What would be your position??!! I just inserted my finger and you are crying like a baby!!! I know you haven't mustrabrated yet because you didn't know which point takes you High.

Prachi - please stop embarrassing me!! She brusted into tears!!!

Rajveer - calm down ( patting her back and massaging her head) I won't do it again till our haldi....

# Her embarassment

-------------------------------------------------------------------------

Prachi - what do you mean? You won't do till haldi? I will not let you do it again before or after that.

Rajveer - ( holding his dick from up of the pants) I'm sorry baby your mother doesn't want you to come into this world!!!

Prachi- are you out of your mind? So cheap!! Please get out !!!!

Rajveer - ahh! After being satisfied you wants me to go? If you little pussy needed me again!?

Prachi- please leave Raj go hell out of here!!

Rajveer - I'm going but my cock will take you to hell don't worry!! Bye see you ( kisses her cheeks and left)

Author pov-

Prachi bolied water in hot cattle and took vapour inside her pussy to get rid of pain. After minutes she got some relief and started dressing herself, called women outside of the room to get her makeup done. Those women were blushing because they were outside when rajveer entered the room , prachi understood it and cursed rajveer for that. Rajveer went to his room , his dick was so hard it started hurting, he went to the bathroom and took a cold shower after masturbating two three strokes!!He dresses himself and comes into the ground where functions have been organised.He wore a light brown kurta and pajama. His eyes were searching for her butterfly.

She just entered the hall and was looking stunning in multicolour lehenga

.

Functions has started.

All of the popular 90s songs were playing

Mehndi laga ke rakhna...Mehndi h rachne wali....Tere Ishq m pagal ho gya dewana Tera re....

Rajveer and prachi had couple dance on tere bin na lenge ek bhi dam tujhe kitna chahne lge hm........

Each and every person danced on their chosen songs... It's almost 1 am , Mrs Rupa gave prachi her kandani golden kada .

And told her to not open until veer gives his gift on first night.She was so shy !!! Mrs Richa rai ( rajveer sister) gave her anklets , and bent down to make her wear that herself.

Prachi - please didi! What are you doing! You are older than me don't touch my feet .

Mrs Richa- Babu this was my one of the dream that I will make my sister in law wear anklets with my own hand . It has been kept for 4 years. Please let me fullfill it.

Author pov-She made her wear that .

Rajveer - I just want to keep her legs on my shoulder and thrust her listen to her anklets . For sure I'll. Take rest as much as you can Mrs rajveer.

Mr Rishi ( richa husband) - what are you thinking?to keep her leg on your shoulder and listen to her anklets rings??

Rajveer-(shocked) no jija ji why would I think that!! I was just looking at anklets!!

Mr rishi- beta I have been married 6 years back so I can hear your thoughts!!! Don't lie.

Rajveer - hmm !! It's looking so tempting!! Isn't it?!

Mr Rishi - of course yes!! Wait I'll call her !!!

Rajveer - haha okay!!!

Mr Rishi - prachi .... Prach.... Come here.

Prachi- (touches his feet) . Yes jija ji how are you?!

Mr Rishi - I'm amazing but I think veer is not okay!!

Prachi- what happened to him ! He's healthy and standing here!!

Rajveer - ( pouted his lip trying not to laugh) she don't know why she has been called here!!

Mr Rishi - Yes he's standing and with him someone else is giving you standing audition ( witchy laugh)

Prachi- whom ?? I can't see!!

Mr rishi- junior veer , if you want, can see !!

Prachi - ( my face turns red hott air is coming inside from my body) I'll be leaving now.

Mr Rishi- wait wait !! I wanted to give you some advice!!

Prachi- yes ! Please tell me

Mr Rishi - I know that rajveer can satisfy any girl in one go but a girl can't satisfy him in a single go. So start having healthy and rich diet. Otherwise you won't be able to handle his wildness!!!

Rajveer - (brusted into laughter) jija ji why are you scaring her!! She is already maintaining 10 hand distance from me.now it will change into km.

Prachi- haha I wonder if no girl on this earth can satisfy him.

Rajveer - I stepped towards her and leaned my face to her face and said "but you can butterfly" to provoke her I kept middle finger in my mouth which was inside her hours ago.

Prachi- I m mad at him he's so irritating!! Okay jija ji bye ! I touched his feet and left.

Mr rishi- you had good choice veer she is perfect for you!!

Rajveer - if she wasn't I would make her.

Mr Rishi - still you have too!! You need to work harder on her body. Hahahha

Rajveer - what do you think? Will I??

Mr Rishi - I know you sale saheb!! You will!!

Rajveer - come on jija ji everybody does that I'll be not new !!

Mr Rishi - hmm, I also worked really hard on Richa !! I want to see you results in 2 months after marriage.

Rajveer - at least don't talk about my sister in front of me jija ji it's very uncomfortable.

Mr Rishi - that's okay veer don't be .

Richa stepped into the conversation!!

Richa- what don't be??

Mr rishi- nahh nothing it's between us. Let's go darling.

Richa- where?

Mr Rishi - you Don't want to sleep tonight? It's already 2am tomorrow is your brothers wedding....

Richa - yes yes , raj come with us.

Rajveer - feeling outward, no dii I'll be there in 5 min I forgot something.( I left)

Richa- what do you think Rishi about their future?

Rishi- I noticed that they both has ego and if I'm not wrong there will be ego clases. Prachi is calm but she has same attitude and ego as rajveer when it comes to her dignity. I don't know how they be settle in this relationship, veer has no control over his anger, he got worst anger ever , can do anything to fullfill his ego. Let's see hope for the best!!

Richa- hmm , don't worry prachi is an intelligent girl she will make everything smoother!! And veer is not an Angy bird , he rearly gets angry but that is the worst. Everything will be managed out.

Rishi- yes!

Author pov-

Prachi and her family went to there home reached at 3am , where else rajveer and his family are on bed . Prachi is worried about tomorrow, and rajveer is excited about it.

Rajveer pov -I won't touch her without her permission now. I don't know why but I have some soft corner for her. I know she maons and get pleasure but I start it with forcing myself on her . That's not good . Every girl has right to decide whether she wanted to get intimate or not , it's her choice.I will get physical to her only when she allows me or ask me to do so.I want her to ruin but I can't see her in pain . She is innocent. She starts crying whenever I bit her suck her it's a rape I can't do that to my own wife !! I want revenge I want to teach her lesson but that's not the right way, she did it unknowingly, it's not her fault.

Author pov-Thinking all this rajveer slept at 4 am.

Note - NEXT CHAPTER MAY CONTAIN MARITAL RAPE, VI-OLANCE, ANXIETY, TRAUMA, FORCED SEX. Please if you are not comfortable don't read it. Let me know if you are loving rajveer and prachi. If you need something to be changed please mention it. I'm a new writer don't know how to write with perfection I'm sorry if something is inapt in this . Hope you understand.

Thankyou for reading stubborn

# Ego wins (+18)



(CHAPTER IS BIT LONGER)

Author pov-It's 10 am , today is the wedding day everyone is excited but except prachi.She wanted to run out of her house, not begin selfish she thought of her parents and dropped the idea.Everyone is preparing for barat.Rituals have been started, there is messy voices crowd in house.

In the evening.....Everything is up to the mark , everyone is waiting for baarat, rajveer hasn't contacted with Prachi today... This surpriseses h er.Horns on the main gate...Baarat aa gyi baarat aa gyi..... Exclaimed in excitement.Prachi heart beats rapidly.Song plays - aaye dhulhe raja gori khol darwaza.....After an half hour all baarat went to the venue.It was simple and sober looks elegant.

Prachi pov- My father took a loan to marry me, With this kinda person. He doesn't know what his daughter is going through he is happy because I'm being married to a high class and reputed family , I'm sure rajveer parents also don't know about his dark side.I'm stabbing my soul, but it's written in my destiny and I have to accept it.

Author pov- All baarat took their seats.Rajveer was wearing faded shades sherwani . He was looking very handsome of course he is but traditional changes looks.

All were murmuring about his looks , he was looking like Greek god to them.

Where else prachi is wearing contrast red colour lehenga.

She was looking very beautiful, can stole anyone's heart.

After an hour they had varmala , prachi just bowed her head all time.Rajv eer understands she is uncomfortable in between these many peoples so he advised brides maid to take her into the room . This shocked her , for the first time he cared for her without saying a words her understood her....

All is set for weeding rituals, all rituals were complete one by one it's 4am now .

Ps - Pinterest

( In bihar Brahmin don't marry wearing lehenga or sherwani)They changed into saree and dhoti , they are keeping their traditions alive.

Tears rolled down when her put sindoor on her head .

Now it's time for bidai. After it's rituals she felt unconscious rajveer held her in bridal style and took her into the car.

( YOU CAN IGNORE THAT PART IT'S WEEDING RITUALS STORY STARTS FROM HERE)

Prachi pov - where I'm????

Rajveer - you are in my house butterfly!

Prachi- don't lie please take me home please ( she starts crying)

Rajveer - calm down!! You got married with me I'm your husband now ,you are my wife, so it's natural you will live with me isn't it!??

Prachi- I held my head it's aching ,I recalled everything I got married with him yesterday....

Rajveer - I held her hand and told you need not to worry I won't touch you until you wanted to let me touch!!

Prachi- seriously, then stay away from me I removed my hand .

Rajveer - as you wish butterfly!!!( I left the room)

Prachi - he's playing mind games with me , he can't touch me now, he knows it that's why trying to list himself in my good books.Well his room is quite luxurious.

He has a swimming pool attached to his room. A big closet and a huge queen size room. A government servant can't afford this much !! There is something fishy!!! I doubt!!

Author pov- Rajveer never touched prachi in these 3 days and slept on couch. Prachi couldn't believe on him , before marriage he was trying to rape her and now all of sudden?? This is not a good sign ( prachi is an overthinker) . Her in laws loves her so much treat her princess.she never felt she is away from her parents.It's the 4th day of marriage and according to rituals today they can be physical.

Prachi- I'm scared what will he do today. It's evening already and we will have reception tomorrow. I had my haldi just few hours ago. It's nothing to celebrate 5 women applied haldi and told me to bath. I got new thing to know that rajveer has insomnia ( sleep disorder) so walls of the his rooms and window,gate everything becomes sound proof with one click. Advance wow!

Richa- Babu prachi, if you need something tell me please it's your first night and you need strength.( Laughs)

Prachi- no nothing ,thank you didi.

Richa- okay than I won't let come any of the person in the room now get rest for few minutes rajveer will be coming.

Prachi- my face burns, I nodded my head,after she left I stand up and ran towards couch,I don't want to sleep on bed today. They wanted to decorate rooms but veer doesn't like this decoration and all .So room is normal as usual it used to be.I wore a simple white night gown, I have been wearing heavy outfits for the past 4 days .

I heard his footsteps , I closed my eyes my body started shivingin I don't know what he will do.

Rajveer - I came inside room I saw her sleeping, she is on couch ohh ,!! This girl . She won't be comfortable there I stepped towards her and thought to took her to bed, I'll sleep myself on couch.I holded her waist to take her in my lap but she slapped me out of no where.!!

Prachi- what are you doing? This is what I was thinking of why you haven't touched me yet!!

Rajveer - I held my anger and said I was not touching her that way . I'm just controlling myself Nobody has ever touched me for the past 10-15 years How dare she slapped me!!!

Prachi- I know you very well , what you thought I was sleeping and you will take a chance to start your cheap deeds.

Rajveer - I can't control myself, Im trying hard but her words are slapping me on my face , I don't want to lose control. Calm down Raj calm down take a deep breath calm down!!!!!

Prachi - I think you got this wildness genetic, your parents have no control over you they made you a monster.I pitty on them . From where you got this much horny Ness , sex addictive in your body? From your father or mother or from your grand parents??? Answer me ????

Rajveer - how dare she , I can't just I can't, I lost control over myself. I holded her face garbed her chin and said a single sentence " I'll show you now , you don't deserve my kindness bitch". How dare she , I want to kill her. I took her hand and throw her on bed. I won't leave her . You wanted to know from where I got this, wait and watch, I'll make you life miserable bitch. How dare you to talk about my family members like that who gave you permission slut!!I controlled myself when you slapped me but how dare you to talk like that haan!! " Tumhari zindgi ko nark nhi bana Diya Maine to mera naam bhi rajveer thakur nhi yaad rakhna".

Prachi - He's out of his mind what he's doing, he said me bitch and slut!! it hurted me!! He's searching for something,I got a chance to run.Why the balcony door is locked, shitt .. my legs are trembling out of fear, I can't move my legs fast , the pool door is also locked !??? How?? Why?? I stepped towards wardrobe he caught me.

Rajveer-

You think you can protect yourself bitch come here and show me you tits!!

Prachi- I can't believe my ears are bleeding what he said just!? I brusted into tears.

Rajveer - I said come here you bitch open your clothes, and split your legs like you do slut!!!

Prachi - I ?? Slut?? Split legs??? My sound of crying became more louder.

Rajveer -So you won't obey your men haan?? I went infront of her holded her waist and throw her on the bed harshly.I searched and got hand cuffs , she is going backwards with her hand, I holded her hand and handcuffs both of her hand tided it into my name craving veer on my bed after sliding matress!!

Author pov-Rajveer is mad at her, after locking her he tore her gown and made sure that every single light is on of his room to feel her what she is going through to make her uncomfortable. He held her right leg and kept it on his shoulder. She is resisting, he spanked harshly on her ass. She screamed louder.He started licking and eating her pussy like a hungry lion she starts crying out of pain. His room glasses are shielding her screaming can't go outside of the room thinking of this he starts more roughly.

Leave me please leave me don't do this to me please - prachi.

Rajveer holded her neck and started fingering her without any prior infor- mation, she cried out of pain.

Rajveer - don't dare to uttar a single word from your dirty mouth otherwise I'll insert my four fingers in your pussy, why are you acting ?? Stop it now?? I know you are enjoying my finger , she scremed again and I inserted my index finger to support my middle finger.She is sweeping like fish , I'm sorry I'm sorry please please I'm sorry sorry sorry........ ( she is screaming in pain) I inserted my ring finger I want to see her in pain , my three fingers are thrusting her taking her to hell , I'm enjoying it .

Prachi - please leave me veerrr veerrr veerrr please sorrryyyy iiii mmmmm sorry ahhh veerrrr pleaseeee ahhhhh please forgive mee maaa aaaaaaahhhhh veeer I will diiiieee ahhhhhhhh veeerrrr sorryyyyyy.

Rajveer - I like you begging beg more bitch beg more, I increased my thrust Speed, her face has become red her pussy has puffed and has also became red.She is in pain with every thrust her pain increases.

Veer leave her and she is in pain she can't hold more and she is you wife afterall.( My heart said)

Don't leave her how dare she talk like that Bout your family fuck her now till her death fuck her( my mind said)

No that's wrong see her condition she is crying in pain Raj , what promise you made to urself?? You won't touch her without her permission leave her( my heart said again)

Fuck her fuck her fuck her rajj comeon today she dares to slap you and talk shit about your family what she will do tmrw? Fuck her ( my mind said)

Author pov -And ego wins, rajveer took his fingers out of her she started breathing heavily . He opened his boxer and took his dick in his hand and started massaging it. Prachi is losing her consciousness .

Rajveer pov- I pinched on her nipples, she is feeling sleepy she can't without my permission. Ouchhh ... She screamed.My dick will show you hell today bitch. I started rubbing it on her clit and in one jerk I tried to push it inside her, but can't I took lotion from my drawer and applied it on my dick and on her vagina. I was rubbing my dick on her clit till then I took her right bud in my mouth and started sucking it , she is not reacting? Why?? I started stretching her bud with my teeth ahhhhh don't......she screamed . I'm satisfied now. I was streching her right boob with my hand sqinging it hardly pinching it .... She is screaming in pain I love this...... my ears are satisfied..... I dick started paining got a sign , I came down took her both leg and put it on my shoulder holded her both legs behind my neck with right hand and with left hand I massaged my dick and inserted inside her pussy in one go out of pain she started rolling her body , she always cry not a new thing. I slapped on her pussy, she again screamed louder in pain her screaming will bleed my ears, I lean down and took her lips in mine started eating it!! Waited for a min to adjust And started moving my dick in her pussy, her legs are shivering , I know she can't hold this pain, but I'm enjoying it , her tightness is getting my dick more hard, I started moving my waist faster than before... I couldn't hear her screams inside mouth, her legs stopped shivering she stopped resisting.I left her lips and looked at her and she felt unconsciousness.......

# pain and pleasure (+18)

A uthor pov-

Prachi couldn't hold the pain of his roughness and felt unconscious.Rajveer was at his peak , trying not to fuck her and pulled out .

Rajveer pov -Poor girl! Can't even take me . What happens if she is unconscious I can still fuck her , but that's not the motive, I want to see her in pain , she can't feel it, but I'm not done yet.Still I pulled out and held my dick in my hands , I barely drank but I needed it now .There is a small freezer in my room , I took a can of bear and laid on couch, while mustbradung I drank it all.Fuck her tightness, I gave myself 6-7 strokes still find it hard, fuckkk herrrr, I need her hole.For the last time I mustbraded hard and cummed .

Author pov-

Rajveer slept on couch while prachi on bed , her hands are still hand cuffed.

In the morning.....

Rajveer pov-

It's 5 am I'm awake!! I saw myself nacked my dick is hard again. It's normal for boys ..hufff...

I sat and looked into the bed she is still sleeping, I need to wear my pant s.Went to my wardrobe and took a black jogger wear that. I came towards her and freed her right hand from the hand cuff..I want to embarrass her, i throw blanket on the floor so that she couldn't cover herself when she wake up.Made coffee for myself, drinking it while starting at her, she got marks all over her body. Her pussy it red yet!!!

Prachi pov-

I tried to open my eyes my body is acheing , my vagina is hurting me it's very bad ... I rubbed my eyes with right hand ,but couldn't move my left hand, I opened my eyes seen my left hand is hand cuffed ,.... I recalled everything about last night... Tears rolled down, I tried to sit but couldn't it's painful,I scremed ahhhh maaaaa .I felt someone staring at me , I looked down he's there that monster,.... He's staring at me , my boobs , my pussy he made me very uncomfortable he's smiling and smrinking like devil.

I tried to cover myself but got nothing, I feel like dead, I couldn't move body into spirals its paining.I took pillows and kept it on my boobs and pussy.

Hahaha.... ( Rajveer laughing like monster)

It's very painful, all of sudden he's coming towards me... Gooddd please save me please...

I'm sorry rajveerrr please I'm sorry sorry please don't do this to me it's hurting already,!! I'm sorry please forgive me please. Do whatever you want to but don't fuck me please veerr I'm sorry - Im cried and requested him.

Rajveer pov -

Im on the bed sitting nearby her , she's begging. Ahh! It's taking me high.I holded her chin and told- shut up.You don't want to get f-ucked?

Nooo -- while shobing - prachi

Rajveer - okay than!! I have conditions!!

Prachi- what!? I'll do whatever it is!!

Rajveer - first you won't wear panties after today's reception, till when I command you to wear it again!!Second - after dinner,I go jogging with dad , so when I come back I want you to  be nacked and on my bed every night without any excuses!!! Third - you won't let any of the men touch your body !! Am I clear?

Prachi- what kind of condition is this ... Please don't do this with me , I'm sorry please....

Rajveer - aahaa!! kya laga tumhe meri Jaan aese he chor dunga tumhe? Nahi Tod dunga tumhe!! Shut the fuck up .

Prachi- veer please sorry, Maine jaan ke nahi boli heat of the moment ke wajah se hua I'm sorry I didn't mean to.....

Rajveer - Why am I talking you bitch!!?? You felt unconscious last night let's complete it.

Prachi- veer no nooo nooo please, please ( starts crying)

Rajveer - I wont leave her ! Splited her legs and I moved my hand towards her thighs, noo noo noo waittt, Raj wait , why not to let her fuck herself??

Prachi- please please please please please sorry maaf kr dijiye  I'm sorry please veer.

Rajveer - if you don't want I should fuck you take your hand to clit and started massaging it.

Prachi - please, it's paining there please sorry.

Rajveer - okay than I'll do it myself I took my hand towards her vagina, suddenly she dip her fingers inside it .woww!!!

Prachi -I know I gave very indecent remark on his family, but atleast I don't deserve this treatment!! He forcefully got intimated with me I couldn't bear it and became unconscious, it's hurting I feel like someone teared my vagina wall . Now he's telling me to mustbrade in front of him. I haven't done till date with myself how can I , don't even know !!

Rajveer - why you hand is not moving? I'll show you now how to do remove your hand from there!!!

Prachi- after hearing he'll do it , I'm scared he will kill me with his roughness, i started moving my middle finger on my clit and hole it's painful , ahhhhh but better than he will do.

Rajveer - now slide your finger in your hole do it fast bitch.

Prachi- his words are making me hate myself, with his instructions I slided my middle finger inside my vagina Ahhhhaaaaahhhhhhhh it's paining veeeerrrrrr !!! I brusted into tears after screaming.

Rajveer - I know it's hurting her, I inserted my whole length inside her last night... I don't want to be kind to her but she is really in pain..... I don't know what happens to me when I look into her eyes, yesterday I haven't seen into it for this single reason . I holded her hand and took out from her vagina. She is breathing heavily and sobbing in pain. I held her finger and took inside my mouth... She is shocked!!!

Prachi -What is he doing yukkk!!! Im thankful to him at least he mercy upon me!! I tried to take my finger back he's sucking it chiiii ... So unhygienic.. I dared to ask him keeping my life again in danger... What are you doing it's unhygienic and dirty yuk!!! Leave it!!!

Rajveer - Leaving her finger from my, Either is unhygienic or dirty your every cum weather it's from forced sex or from mutual is mine. Understood that!!

Prachi - I'm shocked he's insane, I told him to unlock me , as im getting late. He hover over me suddenly.

Rajveer - So you want me to unlock you?? First satisfy me!!! either give me blowjob , handjob or let me fuck your pussy and rip it apart choice is yours.

Prachi- I m scared again his dick his screwing from his jogger into my vagina... I wanted to cry as much as I can ... I can't wear his dick inside me it's so big , healthy, venis are always popping out , made is hell yesterday!!! What the hell I'm in , I don't the meaning of hand job and blow job. I said him - I don't know how we do hand or blow job .

Rajveer -

Strange!! What on this earth did I get this girl only ?who never mustubrated , don't know the meaning of it, can't hold my length...

Oh I thought a slut knows how to pleasure her boss... I said to her.

I can see this words hurted her ,she closed her eyes and turned her face on right side trying not to cry hard bitting her lips from inside.

I took my face to her face and kissed her on cheeks, holded her face made it straight and started giving her smooch.

My dick is hardened, I can't mustbrade I want her hole , it will tear my jogger...

Prachi agar tum chahti ho mai tumhe maaf kar doon to let me get inside, and I promise I will be gentle.Otherwise, I will still fuck you but roughly rip your pussy apart choice is yours now.

Prachi - Mujhe bardast nhi hoga veer, bahot dard ho raha , please tell me something else .

Rajveer -No I want your hole right now either you give it your own or I'll take it myself. I won't be rough,it won't pain if you say yes .

Prachi- Marna to hai he khud se maro ya koi aur maare! Tears again rolled out of my eyes.

Please please be gentle I can't hold it. I said to him as yes I'm ready.He opened his jogger.. his cock was straight big , 2 inches bigger, it's pink !!venis will burst now it's so harden popping out..

Itna bada nahi jayega , mar jaungi Mai... Words just came out of my mouth.

Rajveer -(Laughs) Sab tumhara he hai Aaj nhi to kal tumhe he Lena hai , chala jayega just don't panic.

Prachi- I saw calmness in his voice, he was before yesterday. I smiled seeing him , if my pain can fade his anger away I'm ready . I held his shoulder just to show the start now!!.He started kissing me from forehead then eyes, nose and ears now lips He said open your mouth butterfly! I can't believe I heard that I thought I won't listen to it again in my life. I am so happy to see his this side again I opened my mouth he entered his tongue and started exploring my mouth. With my left hand he was carrying my hair from my right hand he was squeezing my boobs. I don't know but this was pleasure for the first time I wanted him to touch me.He left my lips and started kissing and sucking all over my neck and leaving marks.He took my boob in his mouth I moaned veeerrrrr... It was so pleasurable. I don't know why but it is...

He is sucking it gently I took my hand to his head and started massaging it as if he was my baby I'm feeding him His right hand touched my vagina, I raised my hip up in pain and  pleasure.Ahhhh.... I'm  enjoying him.

Rajveer -I'm gental as much as I can be , I love her little moans , fuck anger I want to fuck her now with her permission.I pinched her buds ahhhhhhh.... She moaned.My right hand is on her clit rubbing it making it ready to take my dick inside.

Slow down.... It's hurting.....( She said)

I kissed her belly button I know this is her weak point.She raised her hip again . I started sucking her belly button.. she spread her legs, squishing her boobs, biting her lips.  I turned  back to her face and kissed her lips.To kya iss wife ke husband usse khus kr rhe hain?Bahot -- she moaned in pleasure.To kya ab apko cho****... She put her finger on my lips.Said - Aap Jo krna chahe kar skte Hain .

I kissed her forehead. Bit on her earlobes and went down .She is already wet. I kissed her on the top of vagina and licked her every folding. Ahhhhhhhh ..... Veerr.......she moaned.I sat on my knees and lean my body towards her , took my face to her and said..It will pain at first but after it get adjusted you will in pleasure....I started patting her head with my left hand , while my right hand was smoothly rubbing her clit...

Veerr... slowdown.... She sobs , I recalled what I have done to her yester day....Without wasting time I held my dick and inserted less than half of the length...Veer..veer... leave me.....ah....take that out....  She brusted into tears.I know I was rough last night.I tried to make her calm..Bas..bas ho gya thoda der....I started kissing her softly on her lips...She is resisting with her right hand...Veer...I can't... Please.... She screamed.I didn't move and with a jerk I inserted 2/4 of my length inside her.

Veer...no..no.. please.... please I.. can't ah....take...it...out...ahhhah..veer.- ( she screamed in pain)

Her face turned red, I pulled it out...It's hard, paining I need to release it..I kissed her forehead and told I'll be back went to washroom...

Prachi pov-

It's hurting so much ahhhh....maaa....why the hell I agreed...ahhhaa......He ran towards washroom I saw him in pain I don't know why ?? What happened to him?? I haven't done anything!!!

I started massaging my lower belly to get relief. But I'm satisfied it's okay with this pain atleast he cared about me not about last light, tried to rape me , force himself upon me.I'm tired feeling sleepy..... I holded a pillow on my chest and within a minute I slept.

# Dirty talks..

------------------------------------------------------------

Rajveer pov-I opened the shower to let my heat come down.I masturbated while moaning her name......., didn't remember how many times.Im feeling tired now, but have to go on duty, my leave has been terminated due to some official reasons.

For almost a month I have not done  sex with anyone, I was a womenizer before I met her, but after meeting her  knowingly unknowingly I never ever touched any other women except her.

My dick is fucking hard 24*7.

I took shower and , weared towel on my torso and came out. She is sleeping again?? Oh she must be tired, I know that's wasn't sex but enough for her.I freed her left hand from the hand cuff,She must be feeling hurt, I took a bowl of oil I used to massage myself at night before sleeping, it gives me sound sleep.Sat nearby her waist and applied oil on her lower abdomen, thighs,legs started massaging it she woke up.Holded my hand .

Prachi- kon h ? Kya kar rhe Hain aap? I'm shocked seeing him and scared is he trying to do that again?

Rajveer - calm down, mujhe feel hua tumhe pain ho raha hoga socha massage kr dun!! Don't worry I'm not going to do that for now!( Smiles)

Prachi- What does he mean not for now?will he do it again...? Nahi nahi thankyou mujhe jarurat nahi.Im so scared of him , when his mood will turn off and will start fucking me.I can't feel my legs ,Wearing the pain I ran off the bed and tried to stand .

Rajveer -Hold on!! Wait!!! You won't be able to I'll take you to bathroom.

Prachi- Bhai bhag yar! Kosis karo kuch pehna nhi hai tumne , touch krega , fir hawas jaag gya to ??? Tum kya karogi??Thinking all this I stood up and about to fall he held my waist.

Rajveer -I told you to stop! That's the reason why you always get into trouble!! Learn to listen!!! I took her to the bathroom in bridal style, her heartbeat!! It's very fast!! I can feel it!! She is looking so seducing,  shyness in her eyes , chewing her lips, she is trying hard her breasts doesn't touch my chest!! She is different from other girls, I can't recognise what makes her different but she is.I haven't gifted her , it's ritual to give gift on 4th day of marriage. I forgot to buy it too!! I'll today at any cost.

Prachi - God!! Why I feel so hot!! I felt his abs when he held my waist, he took a bath few minutes ago, water droplets are sliding from his hair to his neck and then to chest , I wonder that's the reason why he easily attract any women!! He's so hott!!I'm not admiring him but I'm happy atleast hes treating me good.

I reached bathroom, I said him to leave me at the door, but her took me inside, made me brush and kept me inside bath tub.

Rajveer -Prachi , take a hot water bath you will get relief, have to go downstairs and reception is at night you have to sit almost whole day and half night.

Prachi- I took a towel ,kept it in the bathtub and wrapped it around myself in and told him..Why do you care even? This all is because of you . I don't dare to see on his face .

Rajveer -You were naked whole night till now I have seen every inches of yours there is no need of towel.And secondly if I have done I will do it again if you dare to make me angry.Take bath I'm waiting outside. Or I should wait here??

Prachi-No !! There is no need ! Thankyou.Pagal samjha hai mujhe ?? yaha baith ke dekhenge Mai keise kya krti hu.

Rajveer - Okay than , call me if you are done.I took her glance from tip to toe .I made my mind ill shower with her today at night after reception, I want to see how mesmerising she looks when water roles down on her body

.

Author pov-

Rajveer went outside and thought to dress himself it's almost 7 am he has to leave at 8 , maid came with breakfast told her to keep it aside and he went to his wardrobe. Where else prachi thought not to call him , and tried to come out by herself, she is feeling much relaxed after bath, still it's paining. She saw breakfast on the table without wasting time she thought to eat it and take a painkiller.

Prachi- I eat my breakfast and took painkiller, I kept it on the table and went for dressing myself, where is he??  Leave it that's good!!, I'm relaxed.I choose to wear simple saree.

▢

Dressed myself, touch up with basic makeup and I'm all ready. I noticed the pill has faded my all pain. I'm feeling so calm and relaxed can walk properly stand properly. Thankgod.

Rajveer -Prachi...prachi....where are you...

Prachi- Heinn!! Why is he roaring ?? What have I done?? I ran towards room. I saw him with painkiller in his hand .I asked what happened?

Rajveer -I saw her, looking extremely beautiful in that saree. I stepped towards her and said...  Ye pills tumne Li hai??

Prachi- Haan!! I was in pain , so I took it . What's the problem in that?

Rajveer -This girl will turn me mad I'm already getting late!!I held her hand and made her sit on couch. And tried to made her understand.... This pills can't be used for these types of pain.Painkiller, contraceptive pills create complications in conceiveing child, I don't want that.

Prachi -I was shocked for a moment he knows this much!?? I can't hold that , I have to stand , sit whole day how will I manage - I cleared.

Rajveer- That's okay!! You should have told me , I would brought you a hot bag, These pills are not healthy try to understand.

Prachi- How can I put hot bag there?

Rajveer -Then you should take hot vapour steam.Listen prachi I held her cheeks with my hand sat on my knees and told her that...You haven't mustrabrated till date you are almost running 23 , you were virgin!! To jab pehli baar hota hai dard krta he hai adjust hone Mai time lgta hai ! kabhi na kabhi to hoga he sab ke needs hote hain, hamari body ke bhi hain!!! Okay I forced myself on you last night I shouldn't have done that, I was mad at you , but want to clarify you that.. Mai apne gusse pe control nahi rakh sakta!!

Prachi- So what does it mean? You will rape me when to get angry ( tears rolled again I recalled pain I was in)

Rajveer -I haven't said that, I can't control my anger, you mentioned I am wild because of my genetics and it hit me . Listen babu... See if we get a cut it will pain ( she nodded) on second day it will start healing isn't it? ( Yes- she replied)!yes!! That's the point.It's your first time , it's my fault I have inserted whole length inside you in one go I'm sorry for that!!!At first it will hurt , from the second day it will start healing. Try to explore yourself with your own , which point turns you on! Which point give you pleasure!! Try to know about yourself.

Prachi -I know that !!!

Rajveer - Seriously?!! Tell me !! If she tell me it will be easy for me otherwise I'll have to discover it myself!!

Prachi-My belly button takes me high, My inner thighs takes me high .

Rajveer -Bas!!  Hufff... I'll tell you messaging your clit takes you High, sucking your buds takes you high, rubbing..( she kept hand on my lips)

Prachi -Please don't it's awkward!!( What awkward I'm shy as hell )

Rajveer -It's not !! I want you to enjoy me , enjoy your body, know the pleasure, sex is not about fucking, nor husband wife relationship is about sex.... You are too innocent prachi I'll have to save you from this world.

Prachi -Ohh why is he so desperate!! He doesn't know his gentle touch today gave me pleasure, he's looking so seductively hot, but his dick .... I think a experienced can't even handle his whole length and roughness. Is he doing something with it? How it can be that big I heard Indian man have almost 4-5 inches!!! I pitty on my poor pussy someday she will have to take that whole inside her .Should I ask him about what he told about hand and blow job??I mumrmerd it that louder he listened it !!! Why the hell always me??!! Shhhahhh

Rajveer -So you want to know about it. Okay so hand job is when you will make me mustbrade or fuck with your hand. blow job is that when you will take my dick in your mouth and fuck it with that.... It's next level baccha!!! You are not even beginner now...

Prachi- Chiii..... In mouth!!! Chii.  Chiiii... Chiii

Rajveer -You will take it soon like I took yours and made you maon.( Her face turns red) . You are so heartless?? How can you???

Prachi- Chii... He's thinking I'll take his cock in my mouth? Yukkk!! He's so disgusting how can anyone take that??Why is he telling me heartless?I asked him- what have I done?ohh I recalled it , few hours ago I saw him in pain!! I said-I'm sorry, I saw you in pain today's morning but couldn't know the reason, what happened?? I am sorry if I did something, you rushed to bathroom!!!

Rajveer -Is she really that innocent? Or trying to fool me around! Yes !! You did something, you are killing our children!!

Prachi- Heeinn?? Maine apne bacche ko mara kab? I didn't even get pregnant!!?

Rajveer -I bit my lower lips tryed not to laugh! Because you don't let me to dilever it in your womb I have to flush my children on regular basis.and that pain was because you didn't let me to ejaculate inside you....

Prachi- I will dig this floor and jump into it!!! He is talking so clingy, why I have asked that shitt!! I'm getting burning sensation on my cheeks and chest.

Rajveer -She is so shy!!! Of course in the morning if I haven't fucked her, have done it now!!! Her every expression gets me hard.Oh!! I'm already late it's 7:50 ,I said her...Prachi .... Mera gussa shant ho gya hai iska mtlb ye nahi hai ke tum conditions fullfill nahi karogi!! You have to still obey me!! You took painkiller without my permission, I will check it's effect today's night, be ready!! I kissed her forehead took a sandwich in my hand and left.

Prachi-What does that mean? He'll again force me ??? I heart is beating fast!! I gave permission today just to calm him down !! God knows how much it hurts when he gets inside me!!!I'll not sleep here I have decided!!!!!!I'll face the consequences whatever it will be but not Today!!!

In the evening....

Prachi pov- I am getting ready for reception party. I am excited but deep down I am in tension what veer said before leaving. I wore a pink contrast saree.

Mrs Rupa - beta , are you ready?

Prachi- yes! maa

Mrs Rupa - Bahot Sundar lag rhi ho tum , I applied kajal behind her ear . And informed her that Aaj veer ke dadi maa aa rahi hai! apke bidai ke din he wo chaar dhaam yatra pe gayi thi, mannat thi unki !!

Prachi- Kon se mannat maa?

Mrs Rupa -Beta veer shaadi ke liye Maan nahi Raha tha uski job 24 Mai lag gyi thi, fir bhi usne time manga to 26 Tak uske papa bole !!! Fir bhi wo shaadi krne ke liye nahi raazi tha to uski dadi ne mannat mangi jis din bahu ghar mai pair rakhegi ussi din wo yarta kregi!!

Prachi- Shaadi kyun nahi kar rahe the? Girlfriend ke wajah se?

Mrs Rupa -Nahi beta , pata nahi !!uski koi girlfriends nahi h aaj tak. Dost sab Hain . Fir tum mili usse , mujhe bahot khusi hai ke tum meri Bahu ho sayad isliye mana kar raha tha!!

Prachi- I touched her feel , she looks tensed!! I asked her what's wrong maa?

Mrs Rupa -Beta, tumhari dadi saas thode purane mizaz ke hainn!! , soch purani nahi hai bas bandish bahot hai, to apne sar se pallu mat girana kabhi bhi. Bahot aese baate bolengi jo sunna aacha nhi lagega tumhe par kya kr skti ho!!

(Richa enters the conversation)Babu wo hampe bandish lagati hain fir aap to pote ke he biwi ho ( laughs).Take a chill nothing going to happen.

Prachi- Hope so didi!! Im sacred.

Mrs Rupa - Nothing to be scared of, she is strict and sometimes she will touch you to know your health ,she is MBBS from homeopathy so make yourself comfortable around her ! Look at her Richa I'll be back!! (She left)

Prachi- Didi I wanted to tell you something can I??if you feel comfortable!!

Richa-Yes ,please tell me!!

Prachi- I'm missing my mom , so for today just for one day can I sleep with you ?

Richa- Hummm!! I think veer has done something I m damn sure!! There is no need to ask , I'll take you to my room after the reception ends.

Prachi-No what he'll do !! Thankyou so much ( hugs her).

.

.

.

. Thankyou for reading, please share your view, I'm a new writer if something is inapt in the chapter I'm sorry for that!!! Hope you understand!!Next chapter might be spicy  Love you

Thankyou so much.

# Touch me more!!!(+18)

-------------------------------------------------------

THIS CHAPTER IS GOING TO BE SPICY AND LITTLE BIT BIG. HOPE YOU ENJOY. THANKYOU

Author pov-Rajveer came and got ready immediately, wearing a set of traditional kurta and dhoti.

Rajveer pov -Where is she!? Jija ji…. Have you seen prachi??

Mr Rishi- No! She might be with Richa I guess!! These ladies …. I haven't seen how Richa dressed herself yet!!

Rajveer -Yes! I haven't seen her also ! Okay we will in venue. Come on let's go .

Rishi- Okay!! You look very handsome veer.. aaj prachi ko Marne ka irada hai kya??..( teasing)

Rajveer -Uski aankho pe Patti lagi hai jija ji , (laughs) dekhegi tabhi to kuch feel hoga…

Rishi- I don't think so… Apne unko bahot kuch feel karwaya he hoga!!..

Rajveer -Karwane aur karne mai difference hai jija ji.... She's so innocent, usse bahot kuch pata bhi nahi hai... Lots of basic things, I don't wanna open everything all at once infront of her......she might feel weried and get traumatized!!!

Rishi- Unbelievable!!! Aaj bhi aise ladkiya hoti hai!??? I know you are mature veer but i advice you to go slow..... These types of women are goddess in this world!! I hope you won't hurt her innocence even in anger or by mistake!!

Rajveer -No jija ji!! I'm trying my best!!! I have done something and I regret it!! But I'm controlling myself!! I lost my sense in outrage!!

Rishi- I know you have done something to her , I know your anger issues, that's why I'm worried about her, I know this also maybe you forced yourself on her !!(I said to me)Don't regret it !! What happened happened be careful now!!! I said to him while patting his shoulder.And we left for Venu it's in our backyard!!

Authors pov-The reception party has been started, greetings, receiving gifts, dinner, music , dance everything was perfect.Rajveer is attending his colleagues and guests, prachi's father , brother, uncle has attended the reception and after dinner they left soon!! Last song was played of the night at 12Am

" □□□□ □□ □□□ □□□  □□□ □□ □□□ □□□□  □□ □□ □□□ □□□□□  □□□□□ □□ □□□ □□ □□  □□□□□ □□ "Reyansh who is one of the relative cousins of rajveer approach to dance with Prachi . He's 1 year older than that of prachi.She hesitated, but requested by him one after another she said yes.

They both went to dance floor and started slow couple dance .

Rajveer pov -Where is she?? Dii did prachi left ?

Richa-No she is dancing with reyansh that pevart!!

Rajveer - What the hell?? Why did you let her ?

Richa- He was insisting her to , it's awkward so she joined him.

Rajveer - I'll see it myself ( in anger)

Richa -Please calm down veer!! Please I'll take her to room okay Just calm down .Dadi maa is back and was searching for you and prachi.

Rajveer - I'm going to meet dadi maa ! Within 5 min I want prachi infront of me otherwise I'll look it in my way!! Take her inside!!

Richa- Don't worry I'm going to do that only.

Author pov- Rajveer left and richa went to prachi said her dadimaa is searching for her to get rid of reyansh!! She immediately broke the dance and came with her. Reyansh tried to hold her but Richa managed to go !!

Prachi- Dii isn't he weird? I mean his touch that's not comfortable!!!

Richa- Why what happened?? Are you okay?? Did he do something?? I'm tensionsied as hell...

Prachi-Noo!! He didn't do something but I felt he tried to squeeze my waist several times, he forcefully hugged me it was so uncomfortable!!!!

Richa-What the fuck!??? Rishi....rishi....(Yes) Come here

Prachi- Dii please leave it ..

Richa - There's no way !! To leave him !! I narrated whole story to him and told him to treat him as needed.

Rishi- How dare he!! Don't worry I'll make sure he won't look at any of the women like that again. ( I left)

Prachi - Dii why did you trouble jija ji...?? It's okay he won't do it again ,I'm feeling guilty!!

Richa-If by any chance veer came to know what he did to you he'll kill him!! He was angry as hell when he got to know you are dancing with him ....

Prachi -I'm sorry!! I should have maintained distance!!

Richa- No!! It's not your fault, he's like that, he tried to rape his own cousin sister..Once he made mms of his sister in law while bathing.....there are so many things... It's not your fault relax!!

Authors pov- Richa, prachi left the venue , rishi treated reyansh with his gaurds , function was over.. When Richa prachi entered into the house, they saw dadi maa sitting in the hall.....Where else Rajveer was in his dogs kennel playing with him ,he has changed his clothes ....

It's actually not a kennel, but a room  he dedicated to his dog .Prachi went near dadi maa and touched her feet while setting on the ground.

Dadi maa- dudho nahao puto falo. Beta veer , idhar aao!!

( Rajveer dadi maa) Ps.-pin

Rajveer - haan aa Raha hu, I walked towards her, ohhh!!! She is here, how dare she disobey my condition , I'll see her in the room!!!!

Dadi maa- baitho yaha, bahu tum b baitho , Richa baith jao baccha!!!

(They all took their seats.)

Dadi maa- to tumlog mujhe chote chote Baal gopal kab de rahe ho?? Bolo Babu!!

Rajveer - bahu seh to paati nhi hai baacha kaha se degi....( I mermered)

Prachi- my cheeks are burning... Jii jab bhagwan chahenge!!

Dadi maa- bhagwan chahenge?? Ya tum log chahoge??

Richa- Dadi is so straight forward don't try to fool her ( laughs)

Rajveer -Pehle bolti thi shaadi krlo , ab kr li to baacha kr lo , dadi maa thoda saans to lene dijiye!!!

Dadi maa- Ek baar mehnat kar lo fir chain ke saans lete rehna, 30 ke ho tum generation piche hai tumhara!!!

Prachi- What the hell is this conversation!?? I'm feeling so weird and shy I'm getting burning sensation all over my body.

Rajveer - Dadi maa aapni bahu ko bhi to boliye !! ( I want to see how she manage replies)

Dadi maa- Choti Bahu koi dikkat hai tumhe abhi baccha krne se??

Richa- It's interesting, I know veer is streching this topic, it's funny to see him acting like dumb , prachi she is so shy !!

Prachi- What should I tell her!?? Nahi dadi ji , par I think mere masters complete nhi hue Hain exams ke baad hamlog plan kar lenge!!!

Dadi maa-Mere pet m Pawan tha ( veers dad)8 month's ka tab mai mbbs ke exams di thi!! Don't make excuses!!

Prachi -Why the hell I'm in this hall!! Ahh!!!! Dadi ji jeisa aap bole!!

Rajveer- Whattttt????? What she said just now???? Is she ready to make babies?She's lying!!!

Dadi maa- okay than! To mujhe agle saal Tak Ghar mai ek baacha khelte khudte chahiye!!

Prachi- Jii!! Mai kosis karungi.

Richa- Akele kosis karne se kuch nahi hoga , veer ko bhi krne Dena hai, sath Mai karna hai ( I teased her)

Prachi - Yarr!! Koi mujhe le jao yaha se Kahan fass gayi hu mai, pure pariwar ko sex se related chiz he aachi lagti h?

Author pov- Richa and Rajveer tried to tease prachi ... While dadi maa gave her hemopathy drops and told her this will help her in conceiveing and will make child healthy, she drank it there and took the bottle without her inner concent.Richa and prachi went to richas room ,wherelse dadi went to her room rajveer helped her to go.Rishi was resting in his room, Richa said him to go into the Prachis room because she will sleep here.Rishi unwanted goes , he was waiting for Richa , for romances but got offended when she said to leave the room. He didn't react with a smile he left.Rajveer after making his dadi rest on the bed left the room, waiting for prachi , he brought waist belt for her as a gift, he wanted to shower with her. And make love.Door knocked.He ran towards it and opened it , he's shocked seeing rishi .

Rishi- Apki didi ne ham dono ke laga rakhi hai!! I'm feeling irritated veer by your sister!!

Rajveer - I m hell fucking angry on prachi , she always does that!! I'm frustrated!! I asked jija ji- why are you irritated on dii!

Rishi- Yar veer! I had some plans tonight I told her there was a surprise at night ,in the morning still she didn't cared!!

Rajveer -I m in the same situation jija ji but I haven't told her that !! Okay don't worry after they sleep I'll take prachi to my room.

Rishi- Are you sure? She won't be offended?

Rajveer - For now I'm offended by her.. let's wait for 1:20-30 than I'll excute my plan.

Author pov-After 1:30 am rajveer and Rishi tried to do what they have thought and got successful. There is a lock in every room with a password,

Richa isn't locked it from inside because rishi is also an Ips officer and can need anything anytime . Prachi is feeling hot , horny didn't know why in sleep?? When rajveer kept her on bed she squeezed her boobs in sleep , touching her Belly , spliting and closing her legs!!

Rajveer -What happened to her?? Is she feeling something? Should I wake her up? She is looking so seductive, she is seducing me .I shook her hand , she woke up by jerk. Are you okay I asked!?

Prachi-Yes I'm! I'm feeling something I don't know! Something hot inside my body!!

Rajveer -Is she arosed? But how? Oh shitt!! That drip dadi maa gave her is that viagra?? Shitttt mannn !!!! Why the hell she did that!??? May be to conceive early!? But that's so wrong !! Without letting her know, without her permission why did she gave her?? I ll talk to her tomorrow,but for now what should I do to her!?

Prachi- What the hell is happening to me!? I'm feeling horny! I want him to touch me , fuck me as hard as he can!! Rip my pussy apart, I want him to kiss him , make love with him!! I can't control why this thought is coming in my mind!?? But I can't control, veerrr- I moaned!!

Rajveer -Oh no!! What should I do she is ......my god..!! Prachi .... Do you want to have it? ..... Yess( she moaned while biting her lips) ... You are under the possession of vigra .. I think you should take cold shower.... I don't want to have sex now she is not in her control, I wanted to have but when she has control over her body...

Prachi- I don't need shower... I need you .... Please........ Help me it's taking me mad ... Veerrrr ( I moaned) I want to have sex , I want him to insert his whole length inside me. I started opening my clothes in a min I opened it I wore a night gown of dii.... I'm feeling more horny now..... Veerrrrr.... What re you thinking..... Mujhe apna bana lijiye veer please, pet Mai ajeeb ho Raha hai dard kar raha.... I need you .... He was at the edge of the bed I held his neck and placed my lip on his lips, I don't know how to kiss but wanted to satisfy myself.

Rajveer -.I know she won't do it if she was in her control, but I can't control myself, too ,....I have to, I can't use her condition to satisfy myself.

Prachi- Veer please, it's my permission I want you to fuck me, take me to clouds veer. I held his hand and kept it on my right boob, and I started rubbing my vagina on his pant upper of his length. Fuck me veer.......I layed my head on crook of his neck and bite his earlobe... Aren't you getting hard ? I'm all wet just for you Rajveer.

Rajveer- She is driving me mad by her body, my dick will rip this nicker, I'm getting high I don't know how to control myself..... I held her waist and moved back unlocking her hand from my neck, I don't want she should regret tomorrow.. it's better that I'll musterbrade as usual.

Prachi-Now I can't hold this, I want him inside me ,to provoke him I said..Okay if you think you are incapable to satisfy your wife I'll please myself with something else.... I knew it before, you can't satisfy me .. I ran and took my thick lip gloss bar and came back to bed.This will satisfy me ..... I said to him ,And parted my legs , folded it so that he could see my pussy very clearly and started massaging it on my clit and on the hole from my right hand and squeezing my boobs left hand .Ahhhh.....huffffff...... it's so so good........

Rajveer -How dare she?? In front of me she took a gloss bar and mustbrading with it!! And told me I can't satisfy her!?? I'll see what happens happens I'll fuck her .I took my clothes off, my dick popped out wanted to rip her pussy, I patted on it I'll take you to heaven. I said.I Hover over her , locked her fingers with mine and threw gloss on the floor which broke down.So.... If you can take.... Aaj to Mai tumhe nahi chorunga, khud Sher ke muhh Mai hath daali ho tum...I started licking her pussy.

Prachi- Mai chahti hu aap mujhe nahi chore.... Ahhhh ...... It feel so good veer.....take me to heaven...... please......yessss.......

Rajveer -I accepted her command, started licking it more fast... faster... ..rough.....my god her pussy tastes so good I started sucking it ......she is sqinging my fingers...

Prachi- Veer....ahhhhhh.....yessss......yesssss....hahaha....it feels sooooo gu uuuuuddddddd........you are so gooodddd in......ittt..... rajveer......

Rajveer -My full name from her mouth takes me high level..... I dipped my mouth more into her core she raised her hips in pleasure.....

Prachi- Ahhhhaaa.....fuckkkk......you are so good.......veerrr.........I'm on clouds, I closed my eyes in pleasure, I'm in heaven his every lick takes me to heaven.....veerrrrr.....

Rajveer- I left her right hand and started thrusting my right hand middle finger in her hole....ahhhhhhhhhh.......veeeeerrrrrrr.........(She moaned)... .It's very tight, feels like vacuum inside it which grabbed my finger so tightly.Im licking her clit while my finger is doing it's work, she kept her hand on my head and started holding my hairs in pleasure.....I increased my Speed of thrusting...

Prachi- Ah..ah..ah..ahhhhhh ......just like that.......yesssss.......yesss...yesss...I started rolling my hips in pleasure.....it feels....so...goodddd. it's hurting but pleasure is of next level....He's rough but I like it ......I want him to be more rough....

Veer.....one more...... please.....and he inserted another....Ahhhhh.... . it's painful......ahh..ahhhh ahhhh.ahhhhh.ahhhh.ahhh.............ahhhhh His strokes increased I'm feeling something in my stomach......yesss...... ohhhh.....yessss.........I released.........I'm not in condition to appolosie him ...I cummed on his fingers.....yes this was worthy.....I want him to fuck.

Rajveer - I tasted her it's so good as her moans are...I licked every bit of it ...I saw her she wanted more but I'll give my dick now..... I leaned towards her face and started kissing her passonitaly little rough....she is holding my shoulder tightly......I kissed her eyes, lips, forehead,nose, bit on her earlobes,I don't want it to be lengthy and rough...it's side effects will have to face her by tomorrow... I asked her are you ready... She nodded....I slipped down on her neck kissed her there gave a bite and came on her nipples... With my right hand I was rubbing my dick in her clit... she's ready it has became very slippery.....I started sucking her nipples,they are of dark brown shade I love it...just like chocolate.....Ahhhhh....yes.....she moaned ..and with this I get inside herVeer....ahhhhaaaaaaaaa...... it's hurting.......( She screamed)I pulled out.

Prachi- Why did you pulled out....I liked it.... Pleasure is more don't remove it....till you are done....or I'm done....let me screme.....

Rajveer- She's so wild today!?!! It's unbelievable......she parted her legs more , and I inserted inside her...

Veerrr.....ahhhhhh.......a...hhhhh I stay stilled for 2 minutes while sucking her nipples....... after that I started moving slowly and softly.....Ahh h.....ahhhh....ahhhhh.ahhhh.ahhhh ..Tears rolled down of her eyes, she's crying but didn't let me to pull out .I kissed on her eyes and started kissing her on lips....I want more .....veerrrr....ohhhhyessss......I dipped my dick more it's half now inside her.... She is breathing heavily....a hhhh....veerrrrr......I'm feeling.....you....inside ...ahhh.ahhhh ............your rr....yessss....ahh.ahhhahhhh.ahhhh.ahhh.ahhh., I started thrusting her. .... I won't insert it more .....With every thrust she is moaning Ahhh h..ahhh.ahh.ahhh.ahhh.ahhhh..i love it....I want more.I was getting on my verge I inserted whole length inside her...ahhhhhhhhhhhhhhhh(she screamed in my mouth) but I couldn't help it .. I need to release no w.....I started thrusting...My room is filled with her moaning, her bangles twirling , sound of trusting....Ahhh..ahhhh.ahbhh.veeertrrrr....ahh hhh...ahhbhh..its hurting......ahhhh.ahhahAh.ah.ah.ah.ah....veeerrrrrrrrr ......dont.....ahhhhhhh....ahhhhhhhhhhh. (she moaning mess)I know it's hurting her but I can't pull out now I increase my Speed can't control and was bit rough.She wrapped her legs around my waist... she's enjoying now.....yesss....veeerrr...ahhhhh.ahhhhh.....ahhhhhhhh.yesss.yess.yesss.yessss.yesss.ahhh.ahhha.ahhhh.ahhh.ahhhh.ahhhhh.ahh.....i was near to release I started thrusting her hard , ahhhhhhhhh......goooo.....slowwwwww.....verrrrrrr.....ahhh.ahhhh.ahh hhhhh.ahhhhhh.ahhhhh...(she moaned in pain and pleasure)Prachiii......

...ahhhhhhh.....I moaned and released my seeds into her.......I don't know how many times she cummed!! The bed sheet is wet by it...under her ass to her thighs...I'm not done yet!!! But it looks like she is tired!!! I asked her... you need one more round butterfly!?!She nodded her head.

TO BE CONTINUED...........(This chapter got a bit lengthy)Hope you enjoyed.Thankyou for reading stubborn.

# Not your fault

Rajveer - I pulled out, her hole was dipping with mine and her cum.... I downed my head to her pussy and started licking it....I licked every bit of it and then gave her a taste of it by smooching.She can't fold her legs ... sensation of mine is still there!!

I asked her ... If she knows how to ride?Prachi-What is a ride? Is that something related to sex...?

Rajveer -Hell not!!! I recalled once my friend told me that I'm very passionate and wild in bed I'll get a girl who won't know how to please me .......I think he cursed me....(Delima)

I don't know how many things I have to teach her!!!

I told her...You have to sit on my cock and fuck me!!

Prachi-It will hurt?

Rajveer -Slightly but it will give you double pleasure after that

Prachi-Okay then , I tried to get up but couldn't!!! I'm tired as hell but I want it more and more...... My heart doesn't want it , but my body needs it.

He held me in his arms and made me sit on his lower abdomen.He shifted to the middle of the bed.And said me to lean towards him so he can get his dick inside me!!I leaned and he pushed inside me....I felt pain...ahhhhhh it's hurting.....

Rajveer -It will be okay.... relax ( I consolidated)I held her both hand behind her waist and locked it with my right hand.And grabbed her head by left hand and pulled her towards me...I know she will screme and try to resist.... I want to give her little pain..... I started kissing her on lips and thrusting her slowly...She is moaning in my mouth...

Ahhhh.ahhh.ahhh.its hurting......ahhhh....I held her hand tightly and dipped inside her more...And freed her lips wanting to listen clearly her moans and scremes....Veer.... it's hurting me.....(She said while shobing)

I know butterfly!!! But you invited me !! Now please me until I'm satisfied!!!

Ahhhh.....she started moving her legs and tried to stand out of my body.I freed my right hand behind her waist...I held her waist with my both hands tightly and started thrusting her... slowly..

Ahhh... veer....you are h..... hurt...ing ...me......ahhhh... leave.....noooo..... ahhhhhhhh.....(She scremed tears rolled down from her eyes)

now she needs me...I sat up and hugged her while my dick was inside her....

It's hurting baby?!!!....yess(she said while shobing)

It's gonna alright..wait for few minutes... After few minutes I saw calmness in her face... And started moving my cock inside her core.

She is skretching my back .... I got a sign she is okay now....I held her waist tightly and started thrusting her bit faster...Ahhhh....ahhh.ahhhh...(she is moaning)I'm going to be rough,I mermered in her ears.

Prachi- Okay!! Im feeling sweet pain inside it but that's worthy!!! I held his neck tightly. He said me to cross my legs on his waist.... I accepted his order...I can feel his length inside me it's touching my Womb .Ahhhh...fuckkk.....he has started ....ahhh.ahhhh.veer-vv---eee--rrr ahhhh its hurting...ouch....ahhhh.....ahhhaaa.... ouch....ahhhh...stop.....ahhhh The beast inside him has arisen!!!veerrr....ahhhaaa.....(I started screaming and  crying in pain)I know he won't stop......veeerrrr.......I'm biting his neck so that he could leave me out of it....It started bleeding but I got no response..

Veerr..ahhhha...ahhhha..ahhhha..ahhhhhhh..ahhhhh.stoooppppppp.......it will rip my pussy apart,has reached into my belly...ahhhhaaa...........I cummed 3 times in 5 minutes....now I'm pleased.......I started bouncing my hip to get it more....

Rajveer -Ohh fuck!!!!! Her tightness!!!!!.... Butterfly don't do this you will be dead.....you are giving fire to arisen monster inside me.....She is bouncing her ass,...with every thrust I'm getting wild.....If she has arisen it she will have to please it....I lifted her leg and pushed her on the bed , holded her by hair and started spanking on her ass...

Prachi-    What    are    you    doing!??    Ouch!ouch!ahh!ahh! Ouch!ouch!veer!!Raj!leave!! ouch!!ahhh!! ouch.He's spanking my ass continuously I cummed again because of the Jerk...I haven't counted how many times I cummed tonight....may be. .....20-30 times.Ahhh!!leave!! it hurts!!! Ahhh!!ahhh!!ahhh!ouch

Rajveer -Her ass has become whole red looks like will bleed now, nowit's time to take a ride.I gripped her hair more in my hand... Took my boxer and tied her hand back of her waist.....Now I'll take you to outof this world!!!I told her while spanking again..ouch!!!! ( I way she is screaming now I think the effect of Viagra is vanishing)

Doesn't affect me I'll fuck her if that is all goan than also.I kept a pillow down to her Belly,And gripped her hair!! This lead her to raise her hips.....

Leave me veer please!!I'm tired!!!( She said while feeling sleepy)

Not now butterfly! Your husband will feed you now !!!I spanked on her ass and inserted my dick into her vagina....ahhhhhhhhhhhh(she screamed)I am getting wild as fuck!!!!I started moving and within few seconds I started thrusting her taking her ability to breathe,speak,maon, screme!!!

It feels so high,so horny seeing her red ass , fucking in her pussy, holding her hair, ahhhhh.......( I moaned)

Ahhhh........hhhhhhHHHHH( prachi moaned in pain and pleasure)

Spank.....

Ahhh... don't...

Spank!

It hurts ahhhhhahhahahahahha

Spank !!

Veer........aahhhhhhhhhhhHHHH

Spank!!

Ahhahahahhahahaha

Spank!!

Prachi- Ahahhaha..ahahhaha...ahhhhha... don't.....ahhhhhh....ahhhhhaa aa...ahhhhha....ahhhhhaaa.....ahhhhha.... it's hurting me.....veeeeeeee.... ...ahhhhahhahahha..He's getting rough and rough and rough..... I can't hold it now .... it's hurting me.....

He's not in his control....he has become a monster, a beast......F rom continues 20 minutes he has been like that....Ahhhh..........v eeeerrrrr...............He spanked me again...... His dick will take my life ........Ouch....ahhahhha...aaaaaaa......ahhhhahhha.....ahhhh..ahhh..ah-hhhh.ahhh.ahhhh.ahhh.ahhhh.ahhh.ahh.aaaaaa.........ahh....I can't hold i t.....from 3 hours I'm holding it inside me....I can't now...... Im feeling sleepy my eyes are down I'm tired ......

It's 5 am.

Rajveer -I cummed 6 times in this 3 hours with uncountable rounds......Im on my verge.....Yessss.......fuckkkkk.....youuuuuu....ahhhhhhhhh and cummed for 7th time....I have to join duty at 8 am .... Feeling tired and sleepy.

I look at her she is already sleeping....I didn't noticed when????

I will not take bath now, I'm worried about her , god knows what will be her condition..... I opened the knot of her hand...Took her and placed her on my chest and between of my legs.Both are necked....and I slept with hugging her...

In morning 7am

Prachi- Ahhhhhhhh!!! Hey bhagwan!!!!My body is acheing like hell, I tried to stand up felt something soft, I am lying on his chest, I slept on him??

It's hurting!! I can't hold it!! Ahhhaa..maaaaa..... I started shobbing I can't hold this pain it's very painful....I can't feel my legs.... it's hurting between the thighs, my boobs, my body..ahhh.I can't hold him responsible, I initiated and forced him to have sex with me!! I don't know what happened to me yesterday!!!!I saw his back was skrechted very roughly .

I tried to get down of bed but fell down.....It's already 7 I'm getting late .... I tried to get up by taking support of bed, but somehow I managed to stand , with very little steps I reached washroom.Took a hot water bath for 10-15 min and dressed myself, went to downstairs, done Puja and everyone was sleeping due to late night function..

I thanked God!! eat some of the biscuits and fruits and took painkiller!!! I needed it as hell now.

Rajveer - Shittt!!!! I'm already late!! Within 10min i got ready myself, I haven't seen her she was not in the room, I haven't done my breakfast and left for office!!!If it wasn't that crucial and something which can be disclosed publicly, I would take leave but it's hidden and private!!

In the evening....

Author pov-Rajveer came from the office, he was very tired as he couldn't sleep, changed his clothes eat the dinner and went for jogging with his dad.He has overtime now due to some official reasons.Prachi took two painkillers in one day in morning and at night after dinner... So that she can handle everything...Richa left for her in laws with Rishi,Dadi maa was very eager to know the results of medicine....When Rajveer came back home he went to his dadis room to know why she gave prachi vigra!?

Dadi maa-Aao aao beta ! Keisa raha sab kuch!?

Rajveer -Understood the hint!! Dadi maa apne prachi ko kon si dawa di thi?

Dadi maa-Jo jaruri thi whi de thi! Maine tumhari maa ko ,tumhare behan ko ,Tumhari bua ko sabko di thi.....

Rajveer -Please!wo dawa kis chiz ke hai?

Dadi maa-Wo hai energy lane ke!! Harmones Level badhane ke , ye sab kuch m use hoti hai, before pregnancy, during pregnancy and after pregnancy!!!

Rajveer -Dadi maa please ye sab dawa aap prachi ko mat diya kijye, usse suit nahi krta!!! please request kar rha hu please!!!

Dadi maa-Kyun kya hua? Beta hemopathy suit kre to kre nahi to side effects nahi hota iska!!

Rajveer -Please dadi maa! Aap samjhne ka kosis kijiye please, ( how should I tell her) wo dawa sab uske liye nahi hai

Dadi maa-Thik hai tum jeisa bolo!! Chalo ab jao choti bahu intzaar kar rahi hogi.

Rajveer -Jii! I kissed on her cheeks said good night and left.I entered the room and went to take a shower usually I take it after jogging!!I haven't seen her yet!!from the morning!!!I wore a towel and came out ,when I looked into and admired my body that she touched looking into the mirror .

When I turned stretching marks all over my back I blushed thinking of yesterday night!!

It's her love towards me.....

I changed into nicker and tshirt.I am waiting for her .... Is she hesitated? Shy? Angry??....she knowingly doesn't come infornt of me??I heard shobbing sound...

TO BE CONTINUED........

# Secrets revealed!!

-------------------------------------------------------------

( Please vote  if you are enjoying stubborn  )

Rajveer pov -I got up from the bed and went towards the balcony! There is a swing in between the balcony, I saw someone there, lights are off !!I stwiched on the light, it was her , Shobbing in pain, lying on swing, by making her body spiral, and a hot water bag on her lower abdomen.

I'm feeling very guilty, It is all because of me!!! I stepped towards her.... Carrenesd her head with my hand, she sat up with a jeark!!!

Prachi-

Who??? I saw him!! I instantly wiped my tears!! I took half painkiller , it didn't affect me that much.... I feeling hell pain in my body!!!I don't wanna irritate him, it was my fault and I don't wanna make feel him guilty!!!I'm feeling ashamed of what i did yesterday!! always resisted him for that and myself did that, was like a slut bitch !! !! I am feeling like whore in myself!!

Rajveer -I sat beside her and asked where she was the whole day? You haven't replied my messages my calls? And I haven't seen you till yet!!!?

Prachi- I turned my face left side lowering my gaze he's sitting right side of me , I just don't wanna recall it what I did...

Rajveer -What happened babe? Are you upset about yesterday? I stood up and wiped her tears off which is continuously falling from her eyes.. I hugged her face and is touching my stomach!!! She held my waist tightly and her shobing turned into crying!!!

I can't see her like that... It's hurting me....Kya hua prachi? Tumhe pain ho Rahi hai? Kal ke liye upset ho? Kissi ne kuch kaha tumse? I'm sorry meri galti hai, Mai kho Diya tha khud ko I couldn't control myself, I'm sorry baccha!!! Kyun ro Rahi ho bataogi nahi mujhe??...I tried to know the reason...

Prachi- My frustrations changed into anger... I leaved his waist and wiped off my tears And said to him ..I'm sorry.....Maine jaan...ke..nahi...kiya ye sab....mujhe ganda ..... ganda.....feel ho Raha hai ....... While shobing and after I completed my sentence I again brusted into tears.

Rajveer -I started wipping off her tears....kissed on her cheeks,sat beside her and hugged her from her shoulder and said...Ismai ganda kya hai?... I'm your husband butterfly!! You can demand anything from me......mujhe aacha laga tumhe dekh kar .......Mai tumhara hun tum kuch bhi kar sakti ho, bol sakti ho mujhe..... Tumhara pura haq hai.....stop crying....Maine kuch bola...mujhe bahot Kushi hue tumhe kal dekh ke... thankyou for that....I kissed her forehead, her tears has stopped...I held her in my hand in bridal style and took her to bed.

Gives her glass of water.... Dard ho raha hai tumhe?....she nodded...Okay than .....I closed balcony gate and curtains with my remote...And took the bowl of oil and sat beside her leg...I started rasing her saree... She held my hand...

Prachi- No!! please.... I will do it myself..pati pair nahi chute!!.( Told him) , it's awkward he will massage my legs!!!

Rajveer -Why you will do it by yourself? If I'm here!!!....kon bola pati pair nahi chute ? Pati sab jagah chuu sakta hai par pair nahi ajeeb baat hai ( I teased her)  it's a request please let me do..... And she left my hand...I held her saree to her thighs, she closed her eyes maybe in shyness!!I applied oil and massaged it for 5-10 min.She removed her legs ...... Are you reliefed?? I asked!! ,yes.... thankyou so much veer....( She said)I smiled.

I kept Bowl to my drawer besides my bed and went to bed nearby her and removed her hot bag, started massaging her belly with my hand..

Prachi- It's so awkward and reliefed he's doing these thing's..... I didn't stop him from massaging my abdomen I needed it now, throwing my shyness and hesitation away.....He laid half , and took my head to his chest, he's holding my left hand with his right hand and massaging my Belly with his left hand ,I'm feeling so relaxed!!!

Rajveer -I should tell her why I'm way I'm ?!! And some of my family dark sides!!? Afterall she is my wife.... She should know about these things.....

Prachi I wanted to tell you something...

Yes please....she said while looking at me.

Please don't judge my family from this, Mai isliye bata Raha hun kyunki tumhe pata hona chiyea meri wife ho tum!!She nodded her head.And I started with her approval...

I'm an ips and my dad is a retired commissioner you know, but the things you don't know is my grandfather was in RAW (research and analysis wing ) as an undercover agent....we didn't know his identity, as it's prohibited in the norms, and my fore grandfather was  from undercover world.... When my grandfather under a mission, he got to know that his father was behind most of illegal activities and attacks happing in the country....He broke down, he got an order to shoot at sight to his father... For his duty, for his nation he killed his own father without thinking twice..... He was depressed not because he killed him but because my fore father was involved in terrorist activities..... After some years he was sent for a mission ,abroad but one of his colleagues got caught by their officers,As per the norms the govt denied his identity... got an order to kill his colleague as soon as possible.....He and his rest team mates successfully completed both missions.When he came back to India...he took retirement and after that out the blue his identity was reaveled...my family was very proud of him, until he was shot in the next morning...He was on his death bed when he told me that..." Beta rajveer, tumhare dada ji ne desh ke liye kaam kiye hain, tumhare papa bhi karenge, Mai chahta hu tum bhi Karo aur tumhare aane wale generation bhi kare... Hame karz utarna hai bharat maa ka , tumhare par-dadaji ek aache insaan nahi the unhone Bharat mata ko dukh pauchya hai, tum khus kroge na apni Bharat maa ko?? ..... I was 10 that time...I didn't know what to tell him... I just nodded and a current flowed in my body I told him... Dada ji mai , meri generation sab milke karz utar denge aap chinta mat karo , aap thik ho jao fir ham maafi bhi mangenge Bharat mata se, apke papa ne sataya hai na bharat mata ko "I still remember, after I left his ICU ward within an hour he was dead.

Prachi- Tears rolled down from his eyes... I didn't know how much pain he holds in his heart.

Rajveer -After that our lives turned up and down due to regular death threats, trying to kill our family, we left our house, escaping here and there, dad result was yet to be out , and after a month he was selected as an ips officer.... It reliefed us to an extent....My dad was broken due to grandfathers death and all of this circumstances.... I started getting anxiety attacks, depression, insomnia all of sudden hit me.... I was hospitalized for 2 months at the age of 11 after discharge I started recovering!!! Even though my father had good income but lived as poor , because his sister lost her husband... He used to give his more than half of the income to her....Me and my family struggled a lot, my father was harrased by underworld, because they wanted him to support from higher authority. When I was at my adultery my friends cheated on me.A girl from my group proposed me , I accepted it because I was also attracted towards her it was not that intense but yet it was!!! It worked for 6 months and than I got selected in civil services at my 24 . She approached me to be physical but I denied because I was not what I was today.One day she and her friends called me for dinner at her home, I went there but they drugged me , and I was not in the condition to resist, she tried to get intimate so that she could charge false claim of rape against me .but couldn't be successful as one of my father's friend was assigned to look after me , because of my background I have always been in danger , he rescued me from there.

I couldn't believe such things can happen to me !! I trusted them .... That was my turn point...... I didn't slept for a week because my problem was arisen of sleep disorder... My room got transformed and all sealed became sound proof and so I did turned into a womaniser and a beast.

Prachi- I couldn't believe!! These things happend to him?!!! This man is so active, with his actions, words,and noticing everything....

It blanked me..... So this luxurious living is because of your fore father..??

I asked him..

Rajveer -No this is ours!!! We left that house while espacing . This is our hard work.. mine , dad and my grandfather.We had our ancestors luxury they used to be thakur..... Kings.In my village and district where I belong to they still consider me as their upcoming king!!Dad donated many things , and developed our village . it's hi-tech as a new generation needed.

Prachi- What is all this? His family connection to underground!? Then as an undercover!? Now kings!? Commissioner!? Hufff..... It will take time to understand prachi .My pain has vanished....due to his massaging.He went through a lot!! That's why he's like this, he has no control on his anger!! I asked him what about your anger issues?

Rajveer -Ahh! That's genetics !!! But they got less than me , my anxiety issue give fire to it. I'm sorry for what I have done till date. I didn't mean to but the devil inside me takes over my mind. I'm so sorry!! You had stuffered because of me. I'm so sorry! I joined my hand leaving her shoulder and massaging.

Prachi- I can't say don't be!! But that's okay it is in past leave it. I holded his hand.And carresessed his cheeks.

Rajveer -Can I sleep on your stomach if you don't mind?

Prachi- I am hesitant! But his teary eyes what else I can do !?? I said him to and I layed on bed.He slided my saree from my belly and placed his face there kissed it and holded my waist and tried to sleep, his body is on my legs, I parted it from my thighs.I started patting on his head and carresess his hair.

He slept in 10mins.

I felt water droplets on my stomach!! He cried?!!! I don't know why!? Holded his head on my stomach and slept.It gives me relief his hot bre athing.This was the first time when I saw his this side.

But I can't forget, how he tried to rape me and he successfully did that, and molested me before marriage!! It can't be forgiven with any of his pain. And I still don't know if he will be like this in future of will again do something which will rip my soul apart.

I slept under him.

In the morning.......

Authors pov- Rajveer wakes up early, he sleeps a sound sleep at night. He saw prachi she was looking so innocent and beautiful... Her mole on right lips were calling him for a  kiss. He controlled himself and wake up !! After freshing he drinks coffee.Taking a little sip he was looking at her admiring her... How much he did to her but at last she win. Anklets on feet making her goddesses

when he saw her waist he remembered his gift and walked towards his cupboard and took that.And stepped towards her she was awakened , he said to her ...come here prachi there is something for you!! She stepped out of the bed and came towards him.He told her If he could make her wear anklets and a waist belt.She first hesitated, and shyed , after she turned around to make him wear that.He touched her belly knowingly she felt a current sensation in her body, to hide it she holded his hand .. let me help you .....she said....he understood what happened to her and blushed....And a pair of anklets. He made her wear that.After she wears he turned her around.

She was looking so sexy.

Rajveer - This is simple.... I bought it Mai chahta hun tum isse roz pehno ... I'm feeling hard again, I want to kiss her passionately and make love with her.Fuck my mind....

# Beast arose (+18)

--------------------------------------------------------------



Authors pov-Rajveer was good enough to prachi taking care of her, making happy, spoiling her with gifts and love, everything was perfect just as an ideal and perfect partner do.... But she was having fear inside which thing would lead fire inside him.... until one day her instinct got right.

At the dining table...

Mrs Rupa -Beta kal leave le lena , hmlog bua ke yaha ja rhe hain!!!

Rajveer -Maa mujhe nahi milegi abhi ek din bhi , bahot crucial time chal rhi hai, aap, dad, dadi maa, aur prachi chale jiyea.

Dadi maa- Nahi!! Sirf ham , bahu aur Pawan jayenge choti bahu nahi jayegi!! Tumhe bhi koi chahiye....

Rajveer -Nahi dadi , Mai thik hu , wo ja sakti hai, baki servents Hain he jarurat hogi to Mai unhe bolunga he na....

Mr Pawan -Nahi beta !! Baat jarurat ke nahi hai , wo newly married hai abhi, aur sabke bich Mai le Jana sahi nahi hoga abhi , log Nazar bhi laga dete hain...

Rajveer -Come on dad.....(Laughs)

Mrs Rupa- Sahi bol rahe hain tumhare papa.... Beta aapko koi dikkat nahi hai na? Aap Jana chahti hain?

Prachi -Nahi maa!! Mujhe gathering pasand bhi nhi hai , Mai janti nhi kissi ko ja ke kya karungi....

Mrs Rupa -Thik hai to final Raha ... Kal hm sab chale jaynge shaadi ke baad laut jayenge fir hoga to reception Mai sab sath chalenge....

Rajveer -Okay mom. I have completed my dinner, dad change your clothes fast I'll be back in 2 min , we ll go for jogging...

Mr pawan- Haan okay !!!

When rajveer left and prachi went to kitchen...

Mr Pawan -Sahi Kiya aap ne!! Abhi veer ko time nahi he milegi 2-3 months honeymoon pe ja nahi skte hain , Ghar m he kuch der akele rahe to sahi rahega...

Dadi maa- Tumhara beta akele kaha rahega.... Aayega raat m , jata hai subha... Time thode spend krega bahu ke sath....

Rupa- Maa!!! Manage kar lenge wo log baache thode Hain!!!Hamne hamara kaam kar diya ab wo log khud samjhdar hain!!

Prachi- Whatt!!!! they are leaving us alone just ,to we can spend time!?Well this is a very developed and understanding thought but I don't want to live alone with him, they don't know their son!!!He hasn't done anything weird in this week but didn't mean he won't do ...... I'm feeling weird, with him alone... In this never ending house??

Hufff leave that.

Author pov- A girl of around 20-22 came , she is the neighbour, Rupa called to company prachi when she is alone.Her name is aashi. She didn't wanted to because had feelings for rajveer, after seeing Prachi behaviour towards her she was happy and choose to accompany her.All they went to their beds for sleeping it's 11 pm.

Rajveer -Do you need anything?

Prachi- No, thankyou. I'll sleep now .

Rajveer -You won't change? I mean it's uncomfortable to sleep in a saree you haven't changed into night clothes after we got intimated last week!!!is there any problem?

Prachi- No nothing, I just don't wanted to, Mai comfortable hun.

Rajveer -Prachi, I'm sorry for what I did, but ek baat mai bolna chahta hu ...

Prachi -Ab kon sa bomb fodna hai?? ( In my mind I said) Haan please boliye....

Rajveer -It's okay agar tum physical nahi hona chahti to , I respect your decision... I won't touch you without your permission,but mujhe nahi pata kab mere gusse pe kabu nahi rahega, I just want one thing from you ....

Prachi- (Indirectly to bol he rahe hain gussa aayega to Mai rape krunga tumhara!!)Haan what do you want??

Rajveer -I'm not possissve but , don't let anyone touch you that way!! I mean thik hai agar koi photo click karwata hai ya normal chiz koi bhi, but I don't want ke koi majak m touch kre... Ya tum usse krne do.... I hope tum samjh Rahi ho Mai kya bolna chahta hun!?

Prachi- Haan don't worry, I won't weise bhi aapke rehte mujhe kon touch karega.....

Rajveer -Haan wahi Mai bolna chahta hun!! Mere rehte , ya na rehte koi aur nahi touch kar skta tumhe am I clear??? Or Else... I took my face towards her face and told...I don't want our first child to born with their mother tears, while getting themselves in Womb....

Prachi- I don't know what to do, I gulped and moved backwards and just told...jiii.....And within a second I turned around showing him my back and slept while covering myself with sheet.

In the morning...Author pov- Rajveer mom.dad and dadi maa is ready to go , luggage has been shifted to car ... Rajveer and prachi touched feet of theirs , and they left.Prachi is feeling awkward, rajveer said her to serve breakfast he will come after wearing his shoes.She served him , he ate and said her to take care ,he may or maynot be late.... She nodded and he left.

Aashi came at noon to accompany her with her 3-4 friends, they all were served with juice , snacks and lunch...After that they went to the pool section, There are 2 pools in the house, one is attached to the Rajveer room which is private on the first floor,where else one is at the ground floor in backyard.They went to backyard for pool party!! Forced to join prachi as well , she wanted to enjoy so joined.All were playing,dancing, eating,joking .Untill rajveer is back home. It was 7 pm.

Rajveer -Prachi kaha hai? I asked to my servent....

Servent -Choti mam saheb, bahar hai pool party chal Rahi hai ...

Rajveer -Wahh!! Kiske sath ??

Servent -Bagal wali aashi aur unke dosto ke sath!!

Rajveer - Aacha thik hai, ek coffee banao Mai aata hu!! I went to see her.... What the hell........how dare he....and how dare she..... Last night I warned her still she doesn't listen.... I'm hell out of my control, a basted lifted her up , she is all soggy in water her saree has sticked to her body showing her body perfect shape, he lifted her up with her waist and thrown her into water.........I don't know what I'll do now,... Uske pass dimag nahi hai?? Koi insaan usko god Mai le Raha hai bheegi hai wo ....how can she?? If she is so enjoying I ll make her enjoy more....

Rama , Rama ......

Haan ji saheb.....(Rama said)

Usko bolo 5 min m sabko veje yaha se...aur pure servents khali Karo within 5 minutes... Late nahi...

Ji saheb ji.(Rama)

Rama - Chote saheb ne bola hai jane ko, mujhe lagta hai choti mam saheb ke sath kuch aacha nahi hone wala hai...

Mam , mam

Prachi- Haan , Rama bolo!!?

Rama- Chote saheb ne bola hai 5 min ke andar sabko bhejne ke liye unke ghar...

Prachi- Aa gye wo? Itni jaldi keise vej du Mai?

Rama- Mam saheb hmko lagta hai wo bahot gusse mai hain, aap jaldi kijiye nhi to wo aur badh jayega...

Prachi- What the hell!??? What have I done!!??I told them , party is over rajveer is back home and he doesn't like this all, because of his work pre ssure... They left after thanking me.When I entered into house I saw him sitting on couch in the hall shirtless!! His eyes.... His eyes are all red!!! All servent vacant house!? Why ?? - I asked him!!

Rajveer-Hmm!!! Because I told them ....

Prachi -Why!??

Rajveer - you will know!! Bahot maza ho Raha tha bahar!?

Prachi -Haan! Bahot aache the sab....

Rajveer -Kal bhi bula lena!! Khas kar ke wo aacha tha na Jo tumhe god m leke panni m fek Raha tha?? I stared her from top to bottom... Fuckkk... Even her nipples are visible......my anger gave fire to the devil inside me.....

Prachi-I don't know I sence something wrong!! He's walking towards me , he's opening his belt... I told him...sab aese he kar rahe the koi mean krke nahi tha...I'm scared I can see he is colliding his teeth, his face and eyes turned are red...what have I done??... Goddd..... please

Rajveer -Koi mean krke nahi kar rha tha? .. ohh.... To thik hai... I won't leave her....her waist can be seen perfectly curved...her breasts size can be perfectly noticed with nipples ... Her belly with my waist belt can seen ....fuck her....I will show her today who she belongs to and who has one and only right to see her like that... She felt something and tried to run ..... Not this.... This will lead you in difficulty....I lifted her and laid on my shoulder went towards my room.

Prachi -Is he psyco?? What does he want??? Agar Mai pool Mai thi to bheegungi he na.. I feel something very bad is going to happen with me... I don't know ... I started beating him on his back but it doesn't effect him .Oh my god!! I'm so scared we reached into room... No one is here to save me from this monster.....goddddd.....I started crying...Joined my hands and said him sorry...I'm sorry I didn't noticed that much please I'm sorry veer please...I kept repeating it but I can't feel any emotion on his face...Beast inside him has arosen....

Rajveer -I made her stand infront of the mirror because I want to show her who she belongs to...Open your saree everything...fast....I commanded her

Prachi -What ??? I'm sorry please please I will not do this again... My tears can't stop...

Rajveer-I'll count up to 10 if you won't , then I'll be not liable for conse quences!!!One.....Two....Three.....Four.....Five .....Tanana......She is all nac ked..... Her waist belt, anklets, bangles and most importantly her Mangal Sutra is on her body.....

Prachi -With whom I'm married too?? This monster,??this womaniser??? Can't he see I'm in pain ?? How can he do this to me??? He made me nacked infront of his eyes!!! How can he??? I hate him!!! Aaj jo hoga wo hoga ... Kal Mai iss insaan se dur chali jaungi iske pass nahi rahungi... He's a devil inside a human body.

Rajveer -I held her hand and made her body turn towards mirror....She can't see herself nacked!!!! She bowed her head!??? Why ??? I wanted to show you !!! I held her chin and made her look into mirror and said...

Agar ek baar bhi aankh niche hue tumhari... Mujhe nahi pata fir tumhara kya hoga.....

She brusted into tears.....I don't fucking care about it .....

I'm on her back , opened my pant and boxer... Held her boobs from her back started squeezing is roughly...Ouchhhh.....ahhhhhh....( She screamed)

Ohh I love this sound!!!Tum kiski wife ho....???She didn't replied....My anger is breaking it's parameter....I left her right boob and inserted my middle and index finger in her pussy..

Ahhhhhhh .....hhhhhh....hhhhhhh ( she screamed)Maine pucha kiski wife ho tum .....

She didn't replied....fuck herrrr....I started thrusting her.... roughly......fu ckkk herrrr......akad nikal dunga Mai prachi.... don't provoke me I said.....

Ahhhh.... hhhh....ahhh.ahhhh ( she is screaming) I again asked her ..Kiski wife ho tum ....Aapki ....she replied.....

I increased my Speed more...she is screaming in pain....Veerrrr ...... leave me......ahhhhhh.....hhhhhhh....hhhhhhh.please.......ahhhhh.im ..... sorry. ....Resisting with her hand , and her legs.

This can't be done babe .....I smrinked Kept my leg on the sitting table which was near the mirror and held her left leg and put it on my leg which was on the table...I will show her now....I started trusting it more roughly my fingers can't be seen properly it was that fast....

Prachi -Ahhhh....hhhhh..ahhh.ahhhh.ahhhh.ahhhh.veerrreeeeeerrrrrr..a hahahaha......soorrrrereyyyyyyyyy.....ahahaa.....I'm a whore to him .... A hhhaaaaaaa..... it's hurting me... . please......ahhhhhhhh.....veeeerrrrrr...... Something stucked in my mind...I won't scream now!!! Even if he fuck me to death!!!

If I!!! that will be my defeate..... Aaj jo karna hai kar lo Mr. rajveer kal se Mai tumhe dikhungi nahi..... I only focused my eyes on the mirror....now let's meet real prachi.... Who is not weak!!! I spoke in my mind and focused on my eyes.... Tears are coming from my eyes like fountain but .....suuuuuuuuu kal Mai iss pinjre se aajad ho jaungi.......

Rajveer-I saw her staring herself into mirror...Let it be.... I pulled my fingers out of her and started licking it....

She tastes same as of first time... I held my dick and started rubbing on her clit in a jerk I pushed into her...She didn't't scremed!???? How????? Why???? I saw a smrinking smile on her face.... Just as hell and witchy.... It gets me more angry and I started thrusting her.....Her whole body is shaking...her boobs are going up and down with every thrust...ahhh...I like it....to give her more I started rubbing her vagina from the top and rough-ness my Speed...Fuckkk.....herrrr...she is so tight....... Her tightness.....oh my god......Now she brusted into tears... crying....

With one hand I'm rubbing her vagina grabbing her, and with left hand I'm spanking on her ass....

Who's your husband...??You...ahhhh...( She replied)

My roughness increased more...She start-ed screaming...Veeeerrrrrr.....ahhh.ahhhh.ahhhhhAhhhhhhhhhhhhh.ah hhh.ahhhha..hahhhahahhahaha.. don't ahhh.ahhhh.ahhhha..ahhh.ahhh h.ahhhh.ahhhhhI love her screaming while I fuck her!!

Don't..... don't.... do....Ahhhhha..ahhhhhhhhhAhhhh.ahhhh.ahhhh.ah hhh veerrrre....And I left her.... No I didn't I don't want to ejaculate inside her... That's the reason....My juice is spread whole over her ass....

She can't stand she was about to fall....I holded her and made her laid on the floor....

Now it's gonna be fun!!! Sweetheart!!!I holded her hand and locked her fingers into mine...Spreaded her legs and started sucking her boobs.... Feed me.....I told her,

Her eyes are focused on celling,... I bit on her nipples to divert her concen-tration ahh... She said and turned her head to the left side while tears are rolling continuously from her eyes......I freed her right hand and put my dick in her pussy half and again locked her with mine.

Shhhhhhh.....( She scremed lower)I pushed my waist and my whole length is inside her.... Ahhhhhh hhhhhh she scremed lowder...

I started thrusting her hard ,whole room is filled with the sound of thrust, and her anklets....In between with her screme and moans....Uffff.........ahhhhhhhhhhhh.ahhh.ahhh.ahhhh.ahhh.ahhh.ahhh.ahhh.ahhhhhhhhhhh..ahhhh ( she scremed again)

I asked her Who's your husband babe..?She didn't replied...I rolled my waist so that my dick can roll inside her...Ahhhhhhhhh...youuuuu...you uuu...youuu are my husband.( She screamed in pain)

To tumhe aese kon dekh skta hai....Aap .....sirf....aap( she is crying her words are not cleared)

Tumhe weise Chuuu kon sakta hai..?Aap .....ahhhhaaaaaa.....ahhhhhha. sirf aap( she said again with a screme)

To usne tumhe keise chua?Galt.....ii.....se........ahhhhhhhhhaaaaahhhhhh( she said)

Aise galti hogi fir..??Nahi.....ahha...ahhh..ahhhha......

I stopped rolling my waist and started fucking her

.....ahhhhh.ahhhhhh.ahhhhh.ahhhhh.ahhhhhh.ahhhhhha.hhhhhhh-hhhjh....aaaaaaaaaa.......hhhhhhhhhhhhhAnd I cummed pulling it out on her pussy and on her boobs.....Im so satisfied seeing her covered in my juice....

I stood up and held her in bridal style towards bathroom....It's last step .....To show her whom.she belongs to....I made her stand by holding wall and turned on shower....Washed off my juices on her body, and her vaginal every folding....Now it's last round.I said her to be on four!! But again she doesn't know anything....

I took her into bath tub kept her body from her belly up of the tub and her lower part in the tub....I sat into tub, pulled her towards me and held her waist tightly while her back touches my chest....Dipped my dick again inside her pussy....and started trusting her....

Ahhhhhhhhh....ahhhhhhhha.hhhhhhh.ahhh.ahhhhh.ahhhha.hahhhha.a hhhhh.ahhhhh.hhhhh.ahhhh.aaahhh.ahhh...........dont...........ahhhhhhh h...hhhh.....ahhhhhhh...ahhhhhha.......ahh.ahhhh.ahhhhh.aaaaaaaaaaahh hhhhhhhhhhhhhhh.I fucked her for 10-15 minutes , she didn't have now energy to scream,

Who's your husband....?She didn't replied....I started rubbing her clit roughly with my left hand while my right hand was tightly holding her waist.....You .......ahhhhhhhhhhhh,(she replied,)

Who's your husband?You.... ...ahhhhahhahahaha( she replied)I asked her this 10 times just to make a image if she repeat it what will be the conseq uences.....

I turned her face towards mind while my dick was inside her and fucked her for more 10 min....Her tears are dried...she is screaming in very low

v               o               i               c               e

ahh.ahhh.ahhb.ahhhh.shhh.ahhh.ahhh.aaaa.hhhh.aahh.ahhhh.ahhhh.ah hhh.ahhhhh.ahhhh.hhhh.ahhhh.ahhhh.ahhhh.ahhhhh.hhhhhh.And with the last thrust she fell on my chest and I cummed into her .....She gripped my shoulder with her nails......leaving marks there.....

Her pushishment is over.....

Prachi- I'm not feeling my body , not my legs, my energy is gone, feel like moron....I don't have capability to clean myself and take my body out of the tub..... He has raped me for the second time after marriage....... It's last i smrinked....I won't say anything....no nothing.....He changed water from the tub, filled with new fresh water....Washed me with every proper way...

Wrapped me into towel and took me to the bed...I wish I can show him what he does to me!! I wish if he could feel my pain! I wish if I could change him...I wish if I could control his anger...Once I was depressed from this nightmare and now this nightmare has became my life.... I won't let it ...... I can't let this prachi to be killed...... I will run.... That's for sure and I felt dizzy....my eyes closed......

# call of devil inside him/her

---

Prachi pov-I woke up , feeling my body ache....I'm sleeping on him, he held my waist tightly and I couldn't move....

I'm not going to wake him up , leave it!!! I layed keeping my hand over his chest and my head on my hand.

Tears again..!!! Who cares!!!!? His chest is all covered with my tears.... But I know neither he cares about it nor I....I ll flew away today.... At any cost.....I know that his servants and guards will inform him but again Im ready with my plan B.

Why is he squeezing my ass? I looked upto him.... He's awake...... Such a disgusting person!!!!

I tried to free myself from his grip..... He spanked on my ass...and left me....

But I can't get over him... I tried 2-3 times but failed....He's smrinking after seeing my efforts....

Rajveer pov- She is looking so beautiful... He hairs covered her face just like our first meet....

She couldn't make herself sit ... And colliding again and again to my body....

"Ye jo tum baar baar mere upar gir Rahi ho isko keise lu main???... Shanti se raho Mai uthata hu, I'm getting hard and you know afterwards."....

Prachi- Sheet was over me , I wrapped it all in a second... And didn't respond  him... He held my waist and made me sit with him on the bed . Ahhhhhh...... I scremed in pain... My vagina...... Ouchhh......

Rajveer -Dard ho raha?!! Dikhalo jayda swell ho gya hai?.....

Prachi- What on earth he wants!??.... again I didn't respond to him and tried to get off the bed , I remember that day when I tried of getting up to normal and fell down... So I'm trying to be very slow.... I'm all nacked.... Covered just myself with wrapping sheets... He held my hand...

Rajveer -Maine kuch bola tumse !!! Dikhalo mujhe!!!! Again you are testing my patience.......

Prachi- With a jerk I freed my hand and took a little step towards bathroom... I don't want to answer him at any cost.... He raped me and now asking of my well being!!! Monster......

Rajveer -I don't know what she is up to .... She never did that.... I got out the bed and stand before her.... Grabbed sheets which she was warping around her body to see her if I hurt more or less.....

Prachi- I just don't want it .... Just don't..... it's enough now ......I held his hand and said....Kya dekhna hai aapko..?? Rape krke victim se puchte Hain keise ho tum??? So just don't.......just ...... I showed him my hand ....

Rajveer -Rape!?? Victim??? I raped you??? If that is the scene.....than yes I raped you....so what???... Aur agar Maine bola mujhe dekhna hai to mujhe dikhao prachi..... And I opened it .... She is all nacked again... Fuckkkk.....I was really harsh on her last night.... She got all over mark her vagina is red and swallow!!!

Prachi- I couldn't hold it and brusted into tears.... I know should not tell him this I did..." Bahot maza aa Raha hai na aapko? Mere sath ye sab karke.... Mujhe meri nazro se aapne hazar baar giraya hai.. Mai baar baar uth jati thi , par apne mujhe mirror ke samne Lake kiya....Mai sochti thi aapko anxiety ke problem hai , anger issues hai past ke wajah se....but no ..you are a monster of a devil, you don't deserve me..... That's the reason why not a single person fell in love with you.....aur dusro ke beti ka dard aap nahi samjhte hai na.... I wish I pray ke aapki bhi beti ho uske sath bhi ye ho tab aap pe wo guzregi , wo dard aap samjhenge to mujhe itne dino se de rhe hain aap.....

Rajveer -My hand was raised to slap her....but I holded it ...... This can't be done..I held her chin...Tumne khud aapni beti ko curse Kiya hai prachi..... And I repeat if you dare to do this again mere bacche ke bare Mai kuch bhi bola tumne to Mai bhul jaunga tumse meri shaadi hue hai..... Keise aurat ho tum??? Chi....!!! Kissi ke baap Mai itna dam nahi hoga jo rajveer thakur k beti ke sath ye sab karega..... Rajveer thakur itna kamjor nahi hai.... Ek baar jabardasti chod kya diya tum apni aukaad bhul gyi ho.... Apni aukaad Mai raho aur apni jagh pe raho ....tumhare liye aacha hoga..

And yes !!! Aaj se tum meri bed pe chiyea jab bhi mai bulaunga kabhi bhi ....jab Mera Mann hoga Mai sex krunga....you have to please me at any cost....not get fuck out of here ......Left her chin with a jeark...

Prachi-

"Bahot hawa hai aapko ?... Wait and watch hawa ke rukh na mor diya maine to mera naam bhi Prachi priyadarshini sorry prachi rajveer thakur nahi .... Yaad rakhna , mera Rona dhona mode deactivate ho chuka hai ... Aukkad kya Mai aapko apke purwajo ko bhi yaad dila dungi.... Bas dekho....aur Rahi baat beti ke ..... To meri beti apni maa jeise to bilkul nahi hogi.....

I said in a very angry tone and witchy voice , left ...fuck this pain..... I held it inside me and walked as normal....

Went to bathroom done with everything, came out weared saare and done Pooja.... And gone to the kitchen. I don't care what the hell he does....I'm not his slave ....

Rajveer -Urr rahi hai bahot ..... Zameen pe lane Mai ek min bhi nahi lagega mujhe isko.... I will look into her after my duty....Im doing my breakfast and will leave now...I went into the kitchen and saw she is looking for something ..

I ordered servants to leave the kitchen by my eyes... And stand beside her, wishpered in her ears...

" Jangal m reh kar Sher se dushmani nahi liya karte , Mai jb aau chup chap kamre m aa jana.."... She turned back!!

Prachi- Mai aapki naukarani nahi hun... Jo kaam hoga dusre se boliye.... Rahi baat jangal ke to Mai Sher to nahi par ye jangal Puri meri hai....

I left kitchen with a smirk....

What does he think of himself!???? Jagah to dikha ke he rahungi Mai.....I'm waiting for him just get out hell from this house...fir m bhi jau iss paglkhana ko chor kar!!!

Author pov-

Rajveer left for the duty without saying a single word to her after that!! Prachi after seeing all chocs went to her room, packed her clothes and was about to leave...Rama is the main servent of the house... She is manager of every servant related to any sector

Prachi- Rama Mai ja Rahi hu.... Chote saheb puche to bolna mujhe nahi pata.... Bas uncle aunty sab ko batana ke Mai Ghar ja Rahi hu thik.....

Rama- Ji mam saheb!!!

When she stepped out of the house rama called guards not to let her out of the mension.....and then called rajveer...

Helllo!! Chote saheb ji mam Ghar se ja Rahi hai......

Rajveer -Usse rok ke rakho Mai aa raha hu...

Rama- Ham bol diye the guards ko , unhe nahi Jane Dene ...

Rajveer - very good.. bas Mai nikal Raha hu...

Prachi- Driver kaha hai??

Guard- Mam saheb wo aayega kuch der m...

Prachi- Thik hai m bus se chali jaungi koi baat nahi...

Guard-Nahi mam ji saheb wo bas aata he hoga thodi der ruk jaye...

Prachi- Thik hai...

After 20 minutes....

Kaha reh gya wo? Mujhe deri ho Rahi hai......

Guard-Bas aa gya mam...

Horns on the gate...

2 guards opened it..It was black Mercedes...she knew this was rajveer...He came out in anger like a volcano  that has erupted just now.....

Prachi-Leave my side!!

Rajveer -Where are you going!? Don't create drama here.....

Prachi -I'm not creating any drama , I'll go and no body can stop me from this...

Rajveer-Before I do something to get I holded her tightly from her shoulder and pressed her venis behind her neck..... She fell unconscious I lifted her and took her towards room..... This is one of a technique which has been taught during training ...

I will do something to her if she remains this stubborn.....I told my servants to look after her , ...mom and dad will be back in an hour...she will be conscious after 2-3 hours.I left .And informed dad , that we had a fight she is angry and will try to go her home back... So just stop her....

Im hell angry on her I'll eat her raw.....

Author pov- Prachi plan was failed which her instincts told her already that it's going to be..... When she gains conscious she saw Mrs Rupa and Mr Pawan besides her....They were taking care of her...

Mrs Rupa -Kya hua beta aapko? Rajveer ne call Kiya tha inko(Pawan) hmlog speed se aaye hain.... Aapki tabiyat thik nahi hai..??

Mr pawan- Aap thik hain ? Aane dijyea veer ko uski class leta hu , himmat keise hue uski apko satane ke....

Prachi- What?? They know the truth?? No!! He's very smart he won't tell them, and played very well hats off to him....He told his parents so that I can't get out of the house..... Good .... Appreciated ...But after seeing his parents I don't want to make them hurt.... They healed my inner child... I'm so greatful to them... But their son...he turned my one night nightmare to my daily routine...... How can he be their child!???...

Mrs rupa-Kya soch rhi ho beta..? Aap tension mat lo ham veer se baat krenge iss matter pe..... Keisa feel ho Raha hai aapko?

Prachi- I came out from my world... Nahi maa ji mai thik hu, wo bas aese he chakkar aa gye the... Jagda unhone Jaan ke kiya hai, kyuki Mai pool party kar rahi thi sabke sath....

I want to give him a mini attack after he comes....

Mr pawan- Pool party aacha!!! Aashi ke sath.... Iss baat ke liye jagra Kiya unse??

Prachi- Ji papa ji.... Mujhse bole Mai kyun gayi? Wo kar rhe the to kar rhe the.... Mai choti jagh se hu mujhe ye sab dekh ke shock nahi hona chaiye..... Apni aadat badlni chahiye.....

Mrs Rupa -Uski itni himmat wo aesa bola choti jagah se hain aap?? Aaj aane dijyea usse..... Aap rest kijiye Mai fresh hoke aati hu thik hai beta....

Her anger can be felt....

Mr Pawan -Uski sangat kharb ho gayi hai lagta hai.... Kuch din se Mai bhi dekh Raha hu alag behave kar raha... Koi baat nahi beta aaj apke samne uski class lunga Mai.....

Prachi- Nahi papa ji !!! Chor dijiye unhe wo gusse mai unse nikal Gaya hoga....

This will act as fuel in fire...His parents are so ground to earth, they love me more than their own children... I can feel that ..... I don't want to use them and involve them but just to show him a simple  glampus of mine side.... I did this .. I'm sorry maa papa ..ji

Mr pawan- Nahi ....nahi chor keise dun ??? Uski himmat itni nhi honi chiyea !!! Ke mere bahu ko ya kissi ko bhi iss tarike se baat kre wo.... I'll see him... Take rest beta .... Im going to fresh myself your dadi maa saas is also worried about you I have to tell her about you condition..... She is waiting...

Rama Rama...

Ji saheb ji...( Rama)

Bahu ke pass raho unka dhyan rakho...

I patted on her head and left....

.

.

.

...

To be continued.....

Next part may be of war......but on bed Stay tuned....Thankyou for reading stubborn.....

# unknown feelings

-----------------------------------------------------------------

In the evening........

Author pov-Pawan and Rupa are waiting for rajveer.... Where else prachi is proud of herself to give a preview of what she can do with him..... Dadi somehow senses what is happening between them....but chooses not to speak.....The door bell rings.... All knew it's Rajveer...... The servant opened the door.... When Mr Pawan was about to speak... He saw rajveer best friend Riya Sehgal.... She has been his friend since childhood but after class 12th she has shifted to different City.... But now she is back and is in the supreme court posted as a lawyer....

Mr Pawan and the rest of the family members welcomed her....Prachi was in the kitchen after listening to some stranger's voice she came out to take a glance.....

She admired her beauty , Riya is a very bold and perfectly shaped girl... Can catch anyone's eyes...

She's feeling unworthy within after seeing riya with rajveer.

Rajveer -Mom Mai khna nahi kahunga, hmlog dinner karke aaye hain.....

Riya-Yes aunty!! Abhi bhi iski pasand same he hai.... Weise wife kaha hai tumhare?....

Mr Pawan -Beta ......prachi.....

Prachi- I hided myself and acted normal as if I didn't saw them and entered into the hall... Haan papa ji...

Mr pawan- Dekho !! Riya aayi hai .... Veer ke childhood friend..

Prachi-I'm feeling so unwanted here!! Kaha wo hai.... Smart, hot and sexy lady kaha mai..... Jii... I stepped towards her.... That monster is staring at me...

Riya stepped forward.... And hugged prachi...

Riya-You are so beautiful my god..... Just like rajveer wanted.... Too sexy Raj chorta nahi hoga tumhe... I said in teasing tone in her ears... She is damn beautiful

Prachi-Nice to meet you.... Chorne ka to nahi pata par himmat nahi hai unki mujhe pakadne ke..... Laugh....

(Ohh... Dinner kar ke aaye hai... Seriously!? Ya ek dusre ko kha ke aaye hain ye log.... Khair mujhe kya bhar Mai jaye....)

Rajveer -Come here Riya!! Mai tumhe room Mai le chalta hu.. purani yaadein taza karte hain...

Riya-Purani yaadein taza karoge to tunhari biwi bahot bura Maan jayeng i......

( Both laugh, and leave for the rajveerroom...

Dadi maa-Isko dimag nahi hai???... Shaadi ho gayi hai uski... Kissi dusre aurat ko kamre Mai le ja Raha hai.... Ghar lane ke jarurat kya thi usse?

Rupa-Maa ji koi baat nahi!! Friend hai uski ... Bahot din baad mili hai to le aaya... Beta tum kha lo ... Jaldi aur kamre Mai tum bhi jao...

Dadi maa-Are bahu khati rehna baad mai...! Uss ladki ke kapre provoking hain... Tum jao wahi pe raho.. ladki ka koi bharosa nahi hai..... Mera pota bhi Kam nahi hai kuch....

Prachi -Dadi ji mai jake kya karungi? Ajeeb lagta hai...

Dadi maa- Mat jao pati ka sez saja do suhagraat ke liye uske sath.... Bewk uff...

Pawan leaves the conversation after listening to his mothers words.... Went to his room and ordered a servant to take his dinner into his room.

Prachi- Tears rolled down from my right eyes... She is telling the truth... If he does something like that what can I do...?? I don't care... But I want to go .

Rupa-Maa ji !! Kya bol Rahi hai aap?? Aise mat boliye aapke beta uth ke gye, prachi ko bhi bura laga...

Dadi maa-Arey!! To kya bolu Mai??? Dekh nahi Rahi tum ?? Uss aurat ko aadha Seena to bahar he nikla hai uska... Isko bole upar Jane to nahi mai jake kya karungi.... Sab ke sab pagal hain....

Prachi- Thik hai dadi maa Mai ja rhi hu !! And I stepped towards my room... I'm feeling so nervous... God.... What the fuckkk....???? She the bitch is laying on my bed..... Why??? Who gave her permission??? Where is that idiot....I asked her...Veer kaha hain??..

Riya- Shower lene Gaya hai... Aao na baitho mere pass... Tumhe pata hai... Phle iss room Mai kitni baar Rahi hun.... Bahot relaxing hai....

Prachi- Haan wo to hai....( Keise nahi hoga 50 baar Jo sex krte hoge tumlog bhkk) Tum kuch logi...?

Riya- Nahi bebes!! Usko aane do fir hmlog movie dekhenge.....

Prachi- Okay!! Tumlog dekh Lena mujhe aacha nahi lagta...( Inn logo ke sath dekhu?? Bich Mai he shuru ho jayenge kutta kutti ke tarah... )

Riya- Nahi fir maza nahi aayega.... Veer ko bahot pasand hai horror movies... Please dekho sath mai...

Prachi-(Sab kuch pta hai isko)..... Thik hai...

And veer came out of the bathroom just in towel on his tornso and started staring on prachi..

Rajveer -Soo!!!! I smell something burning.... Ohhooo.... She!!! Well I wouldn't forgive her what she said today in morning and did.... But this jealousy on her face... Ahhh!! Gives me relief... Let's try how much she can wear this....

Riya....you look so hott.... I mean phle bhi lagti thi..but abhi tk aur jaan mar rahi ho... Kitno ko mara hai tumne??

Riya- Tum to fase nahi... Baki kissi ko fasane ka mood nahi hota.... Laughs....

Prachi- Hehehehe.... Pagal insaan sab.... I don't know but I feel pinching in my heart.... I should leave .... I stood up from the bed and stepped towards the exit of the room...

Rajveer -Aacha hai ja Rahi ho.... Bahot din baad mili hai best friend mujhe thoda privacy chiyea bhi thi..... Smrinked....

Prachi- I can't control myself.... And went towards him still standing on the corner of the bathroom like an idiot.....

I said...Khud ke time privacy chiye aur jab Maine thoda enjoy kya kiya aap.......He grabbed my waist and pulled closer to him , my breasts hit his chest..

He's so so so disgusting..... His friend is laying on bed and he is doing insane things.....Leavvveeeee meeeee....... I tried to free myself but couldn't... His so strong

Rajveer -Kya ?? Thoda sa enjoy Kiya tumne to??? Bolo......... She is feeling so nervous...... These things of her , start doing something inside me.... My all anger is faded.... Can't believe... She is magic.....

Haan bolo to kya bol rhi thi.... Ke maine thoda sa enjoy kya kiya aap....??I leaned towards her right ear and said ...Let me complete... Maine thoda enjoy kya kiya aap ne mere sarir ko tod diya....

Her hot breathing is doing something to me ....... I just don't want to take the chance of falling in love again..... I left her waist..

Riya -What you guys?? Start doing anywhere.... I should leave...

Rajveer -Nhhh! Wait pool party kre?? Tum bhi relax hogi... Aur prachi ko bahot pasand hai....

Prachi- What he is up to???. Im fed up of him...Im leaving..... I have to do dinner...

And I left in 5 sec just don't wanted to be stopped by them...

Author pov-

She went for dinner and done with Rupa and dadi maa... Rupa insisted her to go into the room and tell Riya to sleep in guest room... She went ... She is shocked... Rajveer and Riya are in pool... Riya is wearing her night gown.... Rajveer is in his nicker.....Tears rolled out of her eyes... She started breathing heavily.... And her shobing turned into crying......Rajveer noticed it from hearing her sound but didn't looked back...He wanted to give her the same pain which she has given to him....And all of sudden he came out of the pool and said Riya to come out too...After that he held her waist, lifted her and thrown her into the pool.....After seeing all this prachi shattered into pieces... And left the room

Prachi- I know I don't deserve him!! I don't have that quality ...... How can a person like him marry a girl like me?

He deserves someone better, beautiful, smart, sexy. I'm a loser in everythi ng...... Why am I feeling that bad?? No!!! Don't!!! Please!!! Khud ko dekho koi tumhe keise pasand kar sakta hai??? Koi bhi nahi ..... Kuch hai he nahi aisa.... I should leave them alone and should go to guest room...I wiped my tears ..As I stood up and was to go someone held my hand....

I turned back....It was him...and then she...... Huffff.... Holding his bicep s....

Rajveer -Why didn't you come...? Why your eyes are red??I know she was crying, but let her feel the same pain...

Riya- Bahot maza aaya tum bhi aati na....

Prachi- Meri tabiyat thik nahi hai.... Kal ke wjh s khrb hai... Isliye .... Aap log enjoy kijiye...

Riya- Hmlog ne bahot enjoy Kiya with cold drinks ... I borrowed your gown.. is that okay...?

Rajveer - Haan haan koi dikkat nahi hai... Pehnogi kya tum change krke?? Prachi give your pink saree to her , she will change... And trust me Riya tum bahot aachi lagogi usmai...

Prachi freed her hand and moved towards room ... In anger...

Riya- Yar!! Kyun chida rahe ho? Bura lg Raha hai usse.... Ro rahi thi sayad.... Mat karo aesa...

Rajveer -Mai feel karwa Raha hu bas!! Mujhe keisa lagta hai jab usse koi touch krta hai tab.... Normal ho jayegi kuch der Mai don't worry....

Prachi came with pink saare and gave it to her... Riya wished good night and was about to leave... Rajveer holded her hand and kissed her on cheeks saying that ....

Bhul gayi ham keise good night bolte the....

Riya- Understood him!! Haan haan I gave him a kiss back .... Patted on prachi's shoulder and left...

After that prachi was about to burst in to mixed feelings she held rajveer hand and thrown him on the bed...He was shocked by seeing her this side ..

Rajveer -Woww!!! Just woww!! She also have fire .... Not bad.... That's why she is destined to be my wife.... I'm excited what will she do next...

Prachi- What do you understand yourself??? I don't like these things un derstood.... I sat on his stomach, parting my legs besides....

" Ye sab karna hai to Ghar ke bahar, yaha nahi.... And how dare you to give her my clothes???.... Who gave you permission???

Rajveer -She's looking so hot..... She is on me with her own ... What if she rapes me!?? Ahhh.... Veer... That's not possible.... If she does I'll in heaven.... But it's impossible....She kept her lips on mine.... How can this be possible??? Means seriously???? How....??? I brusted into laughter..... She removed her lips... And held my chin...I can't control myself she is sooooo innocent..... My god how??? How can she be my wife....???

She didn't know how to kiss I know it... But she started biting on my lips???? ( Laugh)

Prachi -Are you mad?? Why are you laughing??Ohh I get it after touching that bitch...." Bahot touch karne ka shoq hai na .... Aaj batati hu mai ..... Mere sath jabardasti krke bhi dusre ke sath maze chiyea??..... Not possibl e...."

I don't know what I'm doing... But today I'll teach him a lesson... I know my lesson will have his pleasure but how dare he to kiss her???????.....I again started kissing him in my way...

Rajveer -(Agar tum aesa mere sath krogi to Mai touch kya rashta bhi badal lunga apna usko dekh ke )...... I held her head and started kissing her back.....She is resting now!!! What kind of punishment is this??..... I again brusted into laughter....

Prachi- Shitttt.... Mujhe to kuch aata bhi nahi hai..... Mai kya krungi yahi mere sath karne lgte hain.....

I don't have any clue what to do , how to do, how to start, from where...

I moved from his stomach... And sat beside him... Again this fucking tears..... I wiped it in a second but it doesn't stoped...

Rajveer -First woman in my life who is this clear, innocent, pure.... How??? In this generation...???? She is crying because she don't know how to sex??? She also cries when I get intimate with her..... !?

My heart is beating different... I don't want to recognise it.... Forced myself on her several times and than I felt guilty... Why I can't control my anger... And what is this way to fuck her without her permission as her punish-ment ....

Held her cheeks... And said....Sorry!! Kya Janna hai tumhe... Mujhe pata hai tum kuch nahi janti ho..... The day I kissed you I knew you didn't know anything and haven't kissed yet, and when i inserted my finger there was blood....

If you want to know something tell me, okay, leave it!! I'll teach you how to do that....

Prachi -I don't want to know, I'll do it myself... Go and teach that bitch Riya...

Rajveer -She is jealous as fuck with her.... Either she admit or not she can't share me with anyone....

No I'll teach you.... Mujhe kaise kya aacha lgta hai ye baat sirf meri biwi ko pata honi chiyea...And I kept my head on her lap ..

To be continued.....

This chapter got lengthy there will definitely be spice  in the next chapter ....

Thank you for all your support and reading stubborn

# confession

----------------------------------------------------------------

Prachi-No that's another thing I'm married to you and being your wife, I feel you should divorce me ,you deserve someone better according to your looks and standard.....I told him while sobbing ..I'm feeling unwanted, unworthy, within myself.... I can't stand beside you.... After all you are married to revenge with me... If it's over, then don't keep yourself in ties.....

Rajveer -What??? I didn't know I hurt you this much....I sat up with a shock..That's not happening in this birth..I won't leave you at any cost.... You are my wife and only you hold that enthusiasm to be with me for a lifetime... It's either you or none...

I'm sorry, I did this knowingly to make you jealous....And I'm extremely sorry for all my deeds....

"Prachi m Jaan ke nahi krta ye sab tumhare sath.... Mai sabke sath aisa he hun.. mujhe apne gusse pe control nahi rehta aur usmai Mai wahi krta hu jisse samne Wale ko nafrat hai.... Tumhe uss chiz se nafrat hai isliye Mai khud ko force krta hu tumpe... Mai change hone ka bahot kosis krta hu par nahi ho paa Raha mujhse.....I'm sorry Mai janta hu ek ladki ke liye uski izzat kitna important hai... I know everything but I can't help please I'm sorry..... Tears rolled down from my eyes... I held her hand and just said..

"Change me please.... Please mujhe change kar do prachi.....I don't know if I have trauma , or some kind of disorder, or ego problem... I don't know anything.... I tried hard to change myself after the day I forced myself on you .... But I couldn't.... The doctor said that a good environment can change my anger issues ... But I haven't got .. I have always been under pressure due to my duty.... I have insomania.... I couldn't sleep for 2-3 nights which triggers my problem.... Please I'm sorry... I know these all are just excuses but I'm sorry.... Please change me.....

Prachi-I know it!! But that's not a reason to rape someone veer.......!! ( I want to tell you about my life, I have been molested, harassed which gave me a phobia I'm scared when someone touches me like that.... And you too are trigging it .... Why won't a wife want to have sex with her husband?? Everybody wants.... But my fear take over it .... I want to break it... I'll, today itself and the day which I feel you should know it I'll tell you)I wiped his tears.

Rajveer- I'm sorry, I couldn't help myself..... I think we should seperate our rooms... It's best way to keep you safe...... If I repeat it a single time more will die in guilt....

Prachi -(If he's that caring... How he can't control his anger.?? He needs someone to take him out of this....)

No need to do it.... We will live in this room and share this bed... That's final....

You know once a priest told me that...." Jis chiz se tum bhagti rahogi wo tumhara picha karti rahegi , tum jaha rahogi wo tumhare piche baithi rahe gi.... Wo badlega nahi tumhe badalna padega"I thought he was mentioning me , but no it's you!!! Mai jis chiz se bhagti hu,thi, wo aap Mai hai.... My eyes became teary.....

Rajveer -Kya hua?? Kis chiz se bhagti ho tum?? I know you fear of sex , but what's the reason??? Is there something related to past???Tell me please.....

Prachi- ( I wish I could but it's not the right time, he's himself in guilt... )Noo!!! Sabko hoti hai first time Mai.... M alag hu mujhe abhi b hoti h... Fake laugh.......

Rajveer -No don't lie , there is something which I don't know..... Tell me..... Please

Prachi- You know everything..... Don't worry...( I just don't want to rise his stubbornness)I kept my lips on his again held his head.... And tired to kiss him...

Teach me how do we do it veer.......

Rajveer -She's unpredictable...... I freeded myself from her grip... I want to know... What is wrong with her...

Tell me .....there is definitely something which I don't know I can sense it....... please tell me....I held her cheeks

Prachi- Not again!!! I think he's my reflection in some cases..... It won't be easy to get him divert....

I hugged him and started kissing his neck..... Pagal aurat kar kya Rahi ho tum??? Tumhe pata bhi hai keise krte hai????I bited in his neck.... Ouch..... prachi (he scremed)I left him to see what happened....

My god it's bleeding..... Fuckk........I stood up to take first aid he held my hand...

Rajveer -Don't !! Just suck it..... And I pulled her towards me She sat on her knees and kept her lips on it... The sensetion in my body.... It's different I'm getting goosebumps.... My heart beat is getting faster.... She started sucking it.... I'm in pleasure... Her single touch made me hard.... What's so different in her?? That makes her unique from everybody....If I didn't meet her I don't know either I would be married or not...She is born for me...just for me....

Prachi- I saw his venis coming up from his hand... He's resisting himself to not take control over me....

He did very bad with me , I don't want any women in this earth faces it... But he has fear or pain inside him of something I couldn't recognise it...... That make him this violent....I removed my lips over his neck..

His eyes are closed.... He's breathing heavily.... Just by a bite???? Hufff...

I asked him..What's next??

What you want to do with me butterfly!??...( Rajveer)

I want to learn kiss !! As you do .... Same to same... I said

Rajveer -Babe its smooching.... I don't think you will learn it that easy but let's give a try...

( What is she doing with me... She knows I can't control myself when she is near me.... Still!??)

Okay see !! We gonna follow steps by step okay!??

Yes...(Prachi)

I gave her trail of 10 times but she hasn't learned it yet!!!

Listen we will do it tomorrow okay!!

Prachi- Noo !! I want to learn it today.... I will do it now..( I just wanted to check , he is really a demon or something inside him makes him !? And he passed.... There is something which triggers him and his anxiety issues)

I learnt it in the second go but just to check I acted fool...Now I'll show him .....

I held his head and another hand on his neck and I started kissing him... His lips are so soft, I tried to enter into his mouth but... As I do, he closed it with his teeth....I smiled after leaving his lips...He smiled back ....

How does it feel to be my wife??( Rajveer)

Horny and arosed (I said)

By my words he opened his mouth in shock.... I think he can't believe what I told him just now ..

I took it as a chance and held his lips and entered into his mouth....Explo ring every corner of it... He held my waist and started kissing me back...

It passed almost 20 minutes....I broke the kiss...

What happened??(Rajveer)

I don't want to waste time on this single kiss.... Tell me something new ...

Rajveer -

She is so horny today!!! It's unbelievable I'm seeing her like this... She kissed perfectly perfect.... I'm hard as hell and want to make love with her... But she .... What should I tell her.... I will go to washroom I can't hold for more.... It's already painful...

I'll be back just few minutes sweetheart.... I told her...

No need to.... She said.I know you are getting hard, I have medicine....

What..?? I mean what do you mean by that??? I said to her.... She is surprising me in every turn....

Prachi -

What I mean,? Don't you know? I want to do it ...... But be slow, I want to learn..... And also tell me the moves which can aries you more.......

Rajveer -Heinnnnnm???? Seriously????? Means sach Mai??? You want to do it by your own????? Prachi ... Baccha aap so jao tabiyat thik nahi hai tumhare....Kiss fir bhi thik tha ye sex karna chahti hai..... Impossible....just impossible.....

Oh my god!! What happened to her!??She pushed me on the bed and sat on my dick.... What she want to do?? She will cry again...

Prachi -M boli na mujhe karna hai.... Aur washroom jake wo sab karne ke jarurat nahi hai..... Im here to satisfy you, please you .... But be gentle it hurts.....

Rajveer -Prachi Mai mar jaunga don't joke with me.... Please.... I don't want to do it ..... You can't handle it ... Yesterday only i did and that was rough....

Prachi -But I want it , yes you did it that's the reason I m telling you to be gentle... I want to feel it enjoy it...

Rajveer,-It's not going to happen try to understand.... I don't want to do it .... I can start gentle but can't end it in that way.... It will again hurt you ... please uthro prachi... I don't want to give you pain now...

What nooo...... Where did she learn it from .....????She is rubbing her vagina over my dick in which she sat few minutes ago... And opening her plates of saree, blouse in a minute she is in her panty and bra....

I can't believe..... She is doing this... That's secondary... Is she doing this without any pressure? Or I flirted with Riya that's the reason,..???

I asked her...Can I know ke aaj meri biwi , mujhpe haq kyun jata Rahi hai?? Riya ke wajah se??

Prachi-Don't talk about her.... I saw porn videos today and I learned few things... They were screaming in pleasure I also want that .... I also want to feel it.... What they were saying!??? ... Ahh...... Yess yess.... Just like that.... O yaaa many more.... I want it ... Give me that pleasure....

Rajveer - She watched porn?? And wants to feel the same?? That's the reason not bad....I told her..If you want so I'll take you to heaven first come down otherwise it's going to be rough...

As soon as I said she came down...I Hover over her... You want to feel it??

Yes ..... ( She said)

Okay than...I'll be gentle I promise, when I get rough tell me... And yes after you starts enjoying I'll be rough....

She held my left cheek and said yes..

I kissed her forehead, to her lips.. bit on her earlobes...She is biting her lower lips.... She looks so sexy....I smiled seeing her expression... It's her first time to enjoy in her sence....

I started sucking her neck... She turned to give me more access... I bite on it ahh... A little moan of her ....

Did I hurt you? - I said

No it's giving me pleasure - she said.

I kissed on her cheeks and went to her boobs opened her bra strap...

And started circling on her nipples just to tease her...

She is frustrated.... I like it... I started sucking her left boob another hand was squeezing her right boobs...

She is massaging my hair in pleasure ,I bite it and she moaned in pleasure...I took my face to her... And said..

Can I use my fingers just to make it ready for my .... she kept her hand on my lips....

Yes use whatever you want... She said.

I kissed on her hand and on her lips, went back to her boobs...Sucking it , biting it .... And my right hand started its journey towards her little cunt...

I entered into her panty.... Fuckkk... she is all wet..... In just 5 minutes.....I parted her vaginal lips and inserted my middle finger, started rubbing her clit gently....I gazed up towards her, her head rolled back and her mouth is open... I slided my finger into her core...Ahhhhhh.....hhh...veerrrrr......( She moaned)Holded my biceps hardly....I left her boobs and went to her lips... Started kissing her.... While my left hand was massaging her head...

Now I started to move my finger inside her....She is moaning in my mou th.....Rising her hips in an interval of 1-2 minutes.....

I leaved her lips and asked her how does it feel??....

Pleasure.... Pain.... heaven..... ( She moaned it)And cummed.... I removed my finger... And started licking her sweet juices....

She held my hand ... It's dirty please don't....(She said)

It's mine....(I said)She downed her eyes in shyness biting her lips....

Are you ready...??

She nodded...I started kissing her from her boobs sucked it one more time and now her belly button..... She gets wild after it....

I started sucking it.... Within a minute she spread her legs and kept it on my shoulder, squeezing her boobs by her own, rolling her hips, rising it up and down..... God..... She is so high....

I removed her panty....And kissed on her vagina top... Fuckkk ....meeee..... veeerrrr.....ahhhhhh..... please ( she is moaning mess)

I started licking her pussy.... She held my hair and started pulling it in pleasure......Ahhhh.....veeerr......I.....saaaidd...fuckkk...meeee......Yesss.....y esssss...ahhhhhhh........fuckkk....meeee....nowwwwww......Fastttttt...... She is moaning.....

I should give it to her now.....I opened my nicker than boxed.....My dick popped out..... Eagerly waiting to get inside her.....

Are you scared of it butterfly??.

No... I want it inside me..... Give it to me..... ( She moaned biting her lips)Her eyes are focused on my dick.... For the first time she demand it from me.....

I started rubbing it on her clit and vagina....

Leaned towards her.... Before telling me, She kept her legs locked on my waist....

Should I??? I asked...

Fasttt....ahhhhh,( she moaned,)

And with a jerk my half length is inside her....

She gripped on my shoulder.... In pain...

Ahhhhhhhh....... it's hurting....ummmmm.....( She screamed)

It won't wait.... I started kissing her cheeks and lips....

Given time to adjust,after 5 minutes....Should I move....,I asked....Yes.....s he said.

I started moving it inside her....Ahh.ahhh.ahhh..ahhhh.ahhhh.ahhhhh... ...hmm.....yesss.ahhh.ahhhh.ahh.ahhhh........ she's moaning

I want whole inside me.... She demanded.....

And again in a push my length was all inside her..

Ahhhhhhhhhhhhhhhhh.....fuckkkkkkkkkk. ( scremed) I waited for another 5 minutes to adjust...

She said to move....I started it very smoothly and softly...

Ahh....ahhhh....ahhhh      ....ahhhh.......yesssss.........ahhhhhh.ahhhh-hh......ahhhhhh.....

Fast .... Do it fast...veer... She demanded.

And I am giving her now in my way.....

I started doing it fast.... Her whole body was shaking even if she was under me.... I'm very conscious about my body .. I lifted it up so that she won't have to keep my whole weight to her ...

Ahhhhh.ahhhh.ahhhhhhhh.ahhhh.ahhh...yesss...yessssss...veeeeerrrrrrr... ..a h h h . a h h h h h . a h h h h h h You . . . . a h h h h ahhhh.are.......yesss...yesss...hmmmmmmm....ahhhh....ahhh.ahhh.Hhh.too o gooodddd......veeerrrrr.......ahhhh.....ahhhhhh....... take.........meeee ......yesss....    that's    the    ........yesssss.......ahhhhhhhh...    it's very.........godddddddd......yesssss.........    Ahhh ahhh.ahhhh.ahhh.ahhhh.ahhhh.ahhahhhh.ahhhh.ahhhhh.ahhhh.ahhhh. ahhh.ahhhh.ahhhh.shhhh.ahhhhh

I don't know how much time she cummed on my dick.....I m on my verge.....

I started it more roughly...

Ahhhh....ah.....slowwww...........ahhhh....ahhhh... it's..... hurting.......ahh hhh..ahhhhhhhhhhhhhhhhhhhhhh........ahhhhhaaaahhhhhhhhh

And I cummed inside her.......This was so fullfilling.....She is tired...... Tears are on the corner of her eyes because of my last thrust.....

Are you okay....??? I asked her while kissing on her forehead...

Yes..... Thankyou..... Raj..veerrrrr....I love you..... (She said)

She said I love you??? I heard it right?? I asked her again what did you say??

I love you Rajveer... I know you don't love me.... Neither I want to fall for you..... But I did.... I love you ...... I know this also you will never ever fall for me ..... I hope ke " agar jadu hota hai to bhagwan aapko mujhse payar karwa de nahi to mujhe apse dur karwa de".....( She said,)

She slept...I admit it or not but I love her .... More than anyone could... But I can't admit it or tell it to her.... I'm a demon she is an angel.... She deserves someone better not me..... I always gave her pain, trauma, and always harassed her, Has a big heart.... Definitely she is goddess who saw something good in me.... And took me as she can love me.... But I am not her type... She deserves a good, lovable, caring husband not me....My words start choking due to crying......

But I can't help it..... I don't want to lose her.... Even if I didn't admitted yet she don't have any expectation from me.... Once I admit it .... My deeds , my anger, everything will be more painful to her.... I know myself I'll do that ...... Devil controls me when I get frustrated..... I don't want to rise hope inside her.....

To be continued.....

.

.

.

..

Next chapter might take U turn in prachi and rajveers lives, something thrilling, exciting is coming....

Thankyou for reading stubborn, and all of your support

..........

# prachi- mistress of don?

------------------------------------------------------------

L EAP....

After 6 months.....

Author pov-The bell rings at 3 am.... A stranger left a card on the door.....
Rajveer opened the door and found no one... looked down and a wedding
invitation card namely '" MEGH WEDS PRACHI "' was laying on floor
........

Rajveer pov-I fell with the shock on the floor and burst into tears......."
Prachiii..... Kaha kaha nahi dhunda tumhe...... Kaha ho tum..... Dekho
tumhara veer kitna badal Gaya hai tumhare liye... Ek baar aa jao... Mai ab
roz Pooja karta hu, Maine apne gusse pe bhi control kar liya hai, jeisa tum
chahti thi Mai weisa ban Gaya hu..... Ab to aa jao...... Tum jeisa bologi ,jo
bologi wo Mai karunga..... Please please aa jao..... Jabse gayi ho mai chain se
soya nahi hu... Maine wo Ghar Tak chor Diya jaha tumhare yaadein hain....
Kitna aur tadpaogi apne veer ko.... Mujhe Janna hai kya tumhara veer itna
galat insaan hai ,?? Kya itna kharab insaan hai?? Jo tum usse itna dard de
Rahi ho....itna tadpa Rahi ho......kitna kosis Kiya Maine tumhe dhundne
ke tum kahi nhi mili ...... Mai mar Gaya hu tumhare Bina bas saase chal
Rahi..... hai..... Her name on the card has ripped my soul.

Author pov-After that the search operation of prachi was re-opened.....
Rajveer has been searching for her like mad in these 6 months, but never
got a single clue..... He is living alone, in a cottage.... Even his sleeping
pills don't affect him anymore....... He has always been in guilt..... Offering
Pooja and prayers both times to God just for her.... She couldn't change
him but her absence did....

Rajveer -At any cost I want him sir!!! He kidnapped my wife....... we have
got some of the clues by this card print....And after digging it we got that
he's an underworld don!!! Engaged in all kinds of illegal activities.....We are
planning to raid him..... Want your permission... I won't leave him rip him
apart....

But sir I want to know why he kidnapped my wife?? If he has enmity with
me he should have done this to me... Why my wife.....?????

Commissioner -

We got the information that he wanted to revenge with you.... Yes!! He has
enimity with you, but the reason of it still unknown!!!

I know you situation rajveer.... But suddenly raid can't be done on his
system... We need a solid evidence and plan to execute it.....

Rajveer -I don't need it sir!!! I'll go all alone myself!! I can't wait more please
sir!!! Tears rolled down from my eyes....I can't hold it anymore....

Sir I haven't seen my wife for 6 months , I have been searching for her
without any clue... You know everything, this brat has kidnapped her....
By knowing all his I can't sit hand on hand please sir... Atleast give me
permission please I beg you sir....

Commissioner -Just wait for two days... We will execute it with all our
force... I know your pain rajveer... But this kind of decisions can't be taken
on emotional basis... He's an underworld don, he has more power, more

influence than us!!! If you want your wife to be saved just wait for two days.... And I'm really proud of you rajveer.... You have given many things for this stysem now it's time to pay back!!!!

Hugged him....

Authors pov- Rajveer couldn't sleep for 2 days , his parents are worried about him as he doesn't respond to them or any other person in his life except his duty ..... He's eagerly waiting for her ... To see her .. to hug her... To kiss her... To let her know how he has changed himself just for her.... To let her know how much he loves her..... to make her feel how special she is for him...He wants to know what happened to her.... Why did she got kidnapped?? What is the enimity of megh with him?? Why he send weeding card to him?? How dare he to mention his love name in that card..... In which situation is she...???In this 6 months not a single day passed without crying, without praying for her well being, without asking for hint where is she...??

She fell for him first , but he felt it harder... But unfortunately she is not here to see how much her rajveer loves her...

On the second day....

He was ready to see her.... His heart his brain was just asking for her.... Time was fixed, operation plan was made... But being stubborn rajveer left 1 hour early he can't wait to see her...

He has inned into their world of crimes.... Wearing just a bullet proof jacket and a licensed gun..... All the technology was hi-tech, he had almost succeeded but sudden smoke caused him to run from there and due to that he got decteded into their radar....

He was bitten mersesly by their goongs , all of his body was covered with his own blood..... He knowingly doesn't counter them back , wanted to take him to megh..... The don of underworld.....

He closed his eyes to act as he felt unconscious, and then according to his plan was taken to megh....

Rajveer -I just want to see you ... I want you to see me feel proud of me... I'm here just for you... prachi"Tum bolti thi mujhe payar nahi hoga tumse???.... Aaj jo haar nahi Manta tha marte dam Tak wo sirf tumhare liye ladne se phle Haar maan baitha hai... Ye payar nahi hai to kya hai...?? Tum ek baar ye jaan lo ke mujhe payar hai tumse, Mai bol du tume, dekh lu tumhe.... Fir agar ye log maar bhi de mujhe koi baat nahi... Team meri tumhe yaha se rescue kar legi ... Uske baad tum free rahogi, mujhse aacha husband mile tumhe....

I was thrown into a hall...It is all black interior , looks like an Kingdom covering all the four side..

Someone said...

"Call sir megh we got him.... Rajveer thakur "

And the second person ran to call him , within a minute a person similar to mine age came and sat on the couch.... With ciggerate in his hand

Sir megh here is that brat!!!- one of person with gun said him..

Ohh!! Thats megh!!! Man who mentioned his name in card!!!

How dare he?? Aaj he to isko pata lgega madhar*hod kiski biwi ko uthya hai....

Megh pov- Chal pille!! Kaha se ips bna re tu?? Haddi feka tu sunghte sunghte aa gya re....

Rajveer -I choose not to speak I just want to see my butterfly , where is she, how is she?? What he has done to her?? She misses me or not...

Megh -Ruk re!! Phle meri chamiya se to mil... Ohhoo sorry urf Teri biwi se.... Re la re usko .... Idhar la....

Rajveer -Chamiya?? He made her his mistress??? What he has done to her?? My heart scattered into pieces and my shobbing turns into crying... What if he forced her? She can't resist!! She has faced lots of pain !! I was not there to save her... I wish I was dead... She must have called me... I couldn't listen her..... I bited my own lips just so that my sound can't be listen by them.....

I winked my eyes with force... To clear my tears ... And saw a women held a girl hand.... I was still on the floor on my stomach... I gazed up ... Wo ... Wo prachi hai..... Kya kiya usne uske sath???!!!.... She is pregnant.... Baby bumb can be seen.... Is that his child?? Why her hair is that short??? I brusted into tears after seeing her just wanted to hug her as tight as possible.....

Why is she running towards him?? Does she loves him?? She hugged him!??. Whyyyyyy? Please kill me somebody.... Please...... I felt my soul out of my body... My prachi...my butterfly hugged someone else with that love??.... But I deserve this... I deserve this.

Megh -Aao prachi , meri god pe baitho.....

Veer aap mujhse bahot payar krte hai.. hai na....( She said in kiddish voice)

Megh- Haan bahot , bahot jyada..... Ab baitho

She sat on his lap.

Rajveer - Why is she calling him veer?? Her tone ,... Her voice tone it's different..... What happened to her.... God please kill me but pardon her... Meri galti ke saza usse mat dejiye please....

Megh- Chal tujhe bahot chull machi hogi sunne ke... Ab tu thoda thoda hosh Mai aaya hai sunn le....

Teri biwi hai na ..... Ab batata hu Teri Jaan ko keise farfaraya hai maine...
Sunnn...

Phle ke tujhe Aaj Tak kuch clue nahi Mila kyuki ye planing ab ke nahi hai
2 saal se ki gyi thi.... Tu kissi se itna attached tha nahi., tera baap hamesha
tujhpe nazar rakhne ke liye ek kutta ko picha lagya tha.... Fir tu ban gya
ips... Mouka dhunte dhunte 6-7 saal nikl gye... Pata chla teri shaadi hue h
, biwi teri ahhhhhh..... Masst hai lekin.... Socha jaan to basti nhi thi Teri
ismai isko chor du... Fir khabar aaya tu payar krne lga hai ... Bas aur kya...
Uss din aayi thi bahar tere bagal wali se milne.... Uthwa liya saali ko ussi ke
Ghar se..... Tujhe kya lgta hai Tera he dimag chalta hai???...

Dekha beta baap baap hota hai tujhe Aaj bhi nhi pta chlta teri biwi kaha
hai...Surprise hai tere liye .... Batau kya.....

Rajveer -Itna ghatiya kaam Kiya hai isne .... Tu dekh na bas beta.... Pura
story suna tu haramzada ... Tab Tak meri team pahuch he jayegi ... Low*de
teri gaa* Mai baas krke ulta latakwaunga tujhe.... Ya fir encounter he hoga
tera.... Randi ke padaish....

But ye prachi....?? Uski aise halat.... Again my eyes started shaading tears....

Megh-

Haan to ye jo baacha hai iske pet Mai wo kiska hai...... Wo hai Rajveer
ka...... Hahahaha.....

Aur ye Mai tujhe isliye bata Raha hu kyunki abhi iska operation hoga .... Ye
baacha niklega tere samne..... Fir isse shaadi krunga Mai...... Jab isko utha
ke laya tha tb he mann Kiya tha suhagraat mana lu..... Lekin tu bhi hawsi
hai sala..... Madharjaat ....

Pura sarir pe tera Nishan tha.... Aur Mai jutha nahi khata.... Socha iske
Nishan hatne ke baad iska maza lunga.... Par mere mann ko Shanti nahi
mil Rahi thi...

To yaha Maine iski saaree utaraayi sabke samne me..... Aur 4 londe ko bola Mai nhi to wo he maza le le.... Par...parrr... Usse phle Maine iske hath mai MEGH apna naam godwaya....

Ye bechari akeli tanha roti rahi... Veer...veerrrr....kaha hai aap.... Please mujhe bachiye.....veerr..chilati Rahi....Mere londe ne isko nochna shuru nhi Kiya ke behosh ho gyi .....

Jab hosh Mai aayi fir chillane lagi.. bagal Mai chaku tha apne hath se mere naam ko mitane lgi... Kaat kaat ke ret liya... Bahot Khoon behne ke karan behosh ho gyi fir.... Tb jake hame pata laga tera baacha iske pet Mai pal Raha hai..... Mann hua gira du fir socha nahi maza nahi aayega thoda bada hone do....

Jab hosh Mai aayi dusre din tab hamari suhagraat ke sez sajayi gayi...mujhe kya fark pdta h Tera baccha jiye ya mare... Mai to krta he uske sath... Jab bari aayi iski to paglo ke tarah karne lagi.... Isse bahot samjhaya ke yaha se bhagna aur Tera yaha aana impossible hai... Fir bhi nahi mani....

Saree khola he tha ke ye do manzila se kud gyi.... Harami aurat.... Dimagi santulan gya iska... Mujhe veer samjhne lagi... Socha aasan hoga isko cho*ne mai... ....Lee nayi baat samne aayi tu bhi iske sath balatkaar krta tha aur tujhse phle bhi iske sath 2 logo ne karne ke kosis ke hai.....


.


..


....


.


.


To be continued......

Did you like this? Please let me know.Thankyou for reading stubborn and all of your support.

# I love you

------------------------------------------------

R ajveer pov-

I couldn't believe my ears.. she was molested before??? That's why she has a phobia!???? How can I do that to her?? .. I raped her .... Molested her harassed her.... How can I ??? Why I didn't understand her.... Why!! Whyyyyy!?!!

Prachi-

Veer veer ye soya kyun hai niche?? ( Pointing her fingers towards rajveer)

Usko bed p sula do.....( She starts clapping)

Megh- Wo abhi hamesha ke liye sone wala hai..... Isliye yahi rehne dete hain...

Prachi- Mai usse dekh lu?? Please please please please...... Hehehe....

Megh- ( Dekh b legi to kon sa pehchangi)

Haan jao...

Authors pov- Prachi stood up from megh lap and started stepping towards rajveer... Rajveer heart is about to collapse, his love is coming towards him even though she doesn't remember anything.....

Prachi came near rajveer and sat beside his head... Rajveer brusted into tears... He wanted to hold her hand.. hug her... Make her feel safe in his arms ...but couldn't....

Prachi- Aaaaa!!! Tumko to bahot khoon nikal raha hai....... Baap re.... Veer iski dawa karwao .... please na.... Isko dard ho raha hoga.....

Megh- Haan !! Iska hoga dawa sb ab....

Rajveer -My eyes forgot to blink... She is near me this near...but I can't touch her .... She is in this position due to me... I hate myself.... My heart will chock now .... I can't see her in this State.... She really forgot me???? Am I really erased from her memory???

Don't give me this punishment please godddd please.... wo mujhse nafrat kre chalega lekin mujhe bhul Jaye??.... Mai keise jiunga....

And she touched my forehead and carressed my hair in back wards.... I can't hold myself now.... My crying sounds was echoing in hall... Why????? Why she??? Why not me??? I just said..... My wife,..... Butterfly....... Prachi....

She removed her hand from my head.... And started stretching her own hairs... Screaming.... Kon ho tum .... Kon hoo...... And she felt unconsci ous.....

Author pov- Prachi while being mentally unstable from past 6 months.... Heard her name from rajveer mouth ... Got some flash back and due to that she felt unconscious...

Rajveer is still layed in the hall... Waiting for perfect time to counter back... Worried about prachi...he tried to touch her face .... But prachi was taken away in the strecher... Megh ordered to operate her and take the infant out of her Womb infront of rajveer.....

5-6 doctors came .... Made setup for operation and gave prachi anesthesia.....

Rajveer is making his gun ready to encounter megh.... He knows that they will check his body so he kept it under his boxer...... Saw time it was 1 pm , his team was to enter....

He has to save himself, prachi and his unborn baby...

Megh- Jate jate sunn to le tujhse dushami kya hai meri....Tere dada ne mere dada ko mara, tere baap se badla lene ke chakkar Mai Mera baap mar gya, ab unn dono ka badla tu, tera baacha , teri biwi chukaayegi....

Rajveer -Chal tera bhi time aagya..... Tere dada ko mere dada ne mara, tere baap ko mere baap ne mara, aur tujhe Maine mara.... And I shot him in between of his eyebrows with two bullets...He is dead in a min... His people started firing but fortunately my team has arrived and shot them dead all...

I ran towards prachi... She's still unconscious and was taken by colleagues before firing, into safer place...

I holded her hand... And felt blur dizzy all around me...... Fell down.... Blank........

After 6 hours......

It's evening... I'm in admitted in ICU ward.... But I don't need it... Where is prachi..?? Where is she???

I raised my hand and a nurse came.... Before listening to me she ran out of the ward....

In a minute my family, dad, mom, my father in law, mother in law,with my colleagues, team and commissioner head.... All were there...

My eyes are only searching for her.... My butterfly..... Where is she...... Is she okay??

Commissioner -Rajveer!! I'm proud of you, but you haven't accepted my command for that you will be punished....

I just smiled.... I want her to punish me, to teach me a lesson....

I asked where is Prachi..... My sound muffled becouse of oxygen mask!!!

Dad came near me to listen it again.... To clear what have I said... But I couldn't complete it felt dizzy and uncousin....

In the next morning -

Mr Pawan -Diwakar ji!! Aap Ghar chle jaiyega hmlog Hain yaha pe.... Jarurat padegi to call krunga m...

Mr diwakar -Nahi mujse nahi Jaya jayega.... Mere damad , meri beti ke ye halat hai ... Mai kahi nahi jaunga....

Mr Pawan started shaading tears....Mr diwakar eyes also cried in pain...

Rajveer -What's time nurse?

( Sir it's 12 pm)!

What?? I was uncosius fir those many hours!!!

Please can you tell me where my wife is??

Nurse -Sure sir!! She is in sock not uttering a single word.... We can't give her electric shock because she is 6 months pregnant.... She is admitted in nearby cabin ward...

Rajveer- What ?? Don't dare anybody to give her electric shock!!! You guys will be dead... Let her be null , but don't dare it!!!...

I started breathing heavily because I was speaking removing my oxygen mask.... My heart beat it's getting faster as it will chock.... Sweat it coming from my forehead in a ac ward... I saw doctors panicking, maybe my pulse rate is going down... I wish I would die..... I want it desperately... This is all Because of me .... She was in hell just because of me..... She felt unworthy because of me.... I never respected her thoughts, her body, her... I wish my life ends here now itself.... I wish I could tell you my butterfly how much I loved you.... You husband... Your lover.... Your soulmate.... Your veer loved you so much..... Tell my child also their father loved them ... But couldn't be with them.... I love you to an extent jaan... Hope if we meet , I'll be the best version of myself... I promise that.... I love you so much my wife, my butterfly, my prachi.....

And doctor gave me an injection... .......

To be continued.....Thankyou so much for reading stubborn

# God gift..

------------------------------------------------------------

Rajveer pov-I heard voices but couldn't respond to it.... I tried to open my eyes.... With lots of struggle I did it.... Long pipelines are injected into my mouth, where I'm? Lots of equipment and machine, are surrounding me....

Where is that nurse? ...... Another one replaced her.... She saw me opening my eyes.... I can see happiness in her eyes ... She is smiling and congratulating me.... Why????

She rushed out , doctors came to check me ... They removed the pipe from my mouth.... I'm feeling free....now.

I told them to remove oxygen so I can breathe myself... They removed the mask and injected a thin pipe in my nostrils....

But I didn't need it...

Door opened..... She .... My wife...... She ran towards me.... And hugged me.... Wait wait... Did she recall everything??

Where is my baby??? Her belly is flat... How??? Did she ?? Did our baby????

I hugged her back with my left hand which could rise only up to an inche. ... I couldn't believe my eyes I have seen her in this form... My old , butterfly is that simple gorgeous saare look... Red bangles on her wrist, Mangal Sutra in her neck, vermilion in her head, small bindi on her forehead, golden tops earrings in her ears..... I have been dead for her this look... I couldn't hold my tears and burst into it.....

She cried too and wiped my tears... I don't know what to tell her ... I don't want to tell her anything now... I just want to see her as my butterfly, my wife, my love I have been craving for months.....

And richa dii came inside... A baby is in her hand.... I am surprised she wasn't pregnant before!! I don't have the guts to ask prachi about our child.... Tears rolled down from my eyes....

Richa-Ohho!!! Dekho betuuuu.... Aapke papa ko hosh aa gya.... Allelele. .....

Rajveer -Is that my ??? My child?? My baby??? My blood??? I want to see... What is it boy or girl??I wanted to touch it.... I asked for it from di...

Richa-I'm so happy for you veer... Tears started shaading from my eyes.My brother has been in a coma for 4 months... I thought we'd lose him.. but God is saviour.... I kissed on his forehead.. and told.

Ye tumhari beti hai one month ke....abhi

Rajveer -I'm shocked 1 month??? I felt uncousious yesterday itself!!

Ek mahina keise hua di? Prematurely hue hai meri nanhi pari kya...??

Richa- I looked at prachi who is sitting beside veer head on the table.... He doesn't know about it we reached to the conclusion....

Nahi ... Tum 4 mahina se coma m the, prachi ka OPD hua hai..... Aaj tum hosh Mai aaye ho...

Rajveer- What???? Mai coma M tha?? Impossible..... I looked at Prachi her hair which was near her ears when I rescued her reached original length as before.... I m unworthy again... At the time of delivery she might have needed me but I was ..... I couldn't welcome my baby to this world.... I'm biting my lips just trying to not cry lowder.....

Author pov- Richa left the ward with doctors just to give them privacy.... Doctor gave reports about rajveer to her that he's fine now had a speedy recovery... And weekenes will remain till months... Only prachi along with Richa was present at that time... As Mrs Rupa fell ill seeing her son in this position... Mr Pawan has to look after her too and changed shifts with Richa and prachi at evening with Mr diwakar. Mr rishi visits quiet often as he can't take leave for this long in his duty.

The whole family members gathered within 10-15 minutes after listening good news about rajveer. Richa holded them out of the ward... So that prachi and rajveer can't be disturbed...

Prachi-I missed you veer!! I missed you so much!!! I thought I lost you... You made me dead.... But I was still having hope that our daughter doesn't deserve this kind of punishment. Eyes filled with tears.

Rajveer - How can you think I can leave you??I'm sorry for what I have done to you!! I ll not repeat it.. I promise that.. If I do you are free to leave me... I love you prachi... I love you .. Mai tumse bahot payar krta hu , Mai bata nahi sakta mere pass sabd nahi hain...

Aese jeise Suraj apni kirno se krta haiAese jeise Chand apni Chandni se krta haiAese jeise Nadi Sagar se karti haiAese jeise shiv Parvati se karte hainWeisa he tumhara rajveer apni prachi se krta hai......

Mujhe laga tumne mujhe bhula diya .. Maine tumhe kho diya... Maine tumhe dard Diya mana Maine... Par tumne mujhe maar he Diya tha .... I cried... I can't believe.... It .... My baby ... My wife.... Are with me.... This is best thing ever happened with me.... I love you... Please don't leave me.... I'm sorry.... Please.... please

Prachi- I know the way you waited for me... I stand up and hugged him tightly as possible it could be with his pipes inserted within his body...

I won't leave you... Never.... I love you more than you love me.......Mai aapko chor k jaungi bhi kaha?? Mujhe marna thode hai..... Mere rajveer ko ye pasand nahi unki biwi kissi ko dekhe bhi to....I smiled saying him this.

Rajveer -Tumhare rajveer ko sab pasand hai... Jo tum karti ho... Jo karna chahti ho... Jo ki ho.... Jo karogi.... Tumhara rajveer pagal hai tumhare piche.....

( Baby cries..... Rajveer has holded har in his left hand)

Areyyy.... Maa ...papa ka romance nahi dekha gaya meri beti ko.... Mera attention chahti hai...... Laughs.

I tried to pick her up towards my face..but couldn't.... Prachi helped me out...

My baby..... My fairy..... My gift..... I kissed her but my bread made her uncomfortable.... I laughed.... She is just like her mother.... Beautiful...just divine goddess.... Calm... Her eyes are on me .... Grey sparkling eyes.... Fair white skin tone.... She holded my face with her little hand... This is heavenly... My daughter touched me for the first time.....

She is looking into my eyes and carresseing my chin.... Again I'm feeling guilty.... I don't know... She is born with my love... Or my obsession.... On her mother???

Tears rolled out again and landed on her cheeks....... I don't know if after seeing her prachi would recall my forced,......her pain.... Her scremes.....

' mujhe nahi pata meri jaan ke tum kab apne maa ke pet Mai gayi.... When I forced her or when it was mutual... But I promise your sibling will be made out of pure love... I'm sorry... Your father is worst person in this world.... But he loves you the most ...... He loves your mommy also but less than you...

She giggled.... Ohh my god!!! That's my daughter.... Hamlog ke khub banegi... Tum apne papa pe jaogi..... I kissed her

Prachi- It's okay veer... No need to dig the past... And I hope.. ke ye apni maa pe nahi jaye.... Koi iski softness, innocence ka fayada na utha sake.....

And what if I don't want second child?

Rajveer -I'm sorry... I'm so sorry... Bhagwan ne mujhe bahot dand diye hain.... Mout aa jaye mujhe lekin ye fir kabhi na ho.... Tumse dur... Apni baache se dur.... ( brusted into tears)

Prachi- He has been changed... Just a transformation.... I love him either the way he is... I held his face kiss on his cheeks.. and wiped his tears off.. . I never thought I would fall for him.....But my heart... It didn't accepted what it has seen... It accepted what his heart hided from the world.... He has been deceived... That's made him a womaniser..... Unworthy of being loved....

My princess also wants kiss from mommy- I kissed her too... She again giggles.... Naughty just like your father I said...

He smiled...

You didn't gave me answer?? What if I don't want second child??

Rajveer -It's all your decision...... I want our children... Our family... With love... With mutual consent... With respect...

Prachi- Well! Mai dekhungi abhi khair aap Mai itni himmat nahi hai ke aap..... Leave it.... Keisa lg rha aapko( I teased him)

Rajveer -My eyes focused on her .... Just on her.... Admiring her... How she forgiven me....and the way she try to teased me...

Himmat ke baat mat karo....tum janti ho... Painkiller Lena padhta tha tumhe.... Abhi bhle he na Lena pade..par itni himmat to hai ke tumhe maa bana saku.....

...

..........

To be continued........Thankyou for reading stubborn.

# Bet (+18)



Author pov-Prachi doesn't want to recall what he has done with her , she took her daughter from his hand and said people are waiting to meet him.. and left the ward after kissing his cheeks...All the family members of both rajveer and prachi with official members were here to greet him congratulations.... The doctor said they could discharge him the next morning....  all are eagerly waiting for his discharge... Rajveer is too , and wanted to go home ,play with her little daughter.... He has been given a bed rest for 2 months.... And is discharged in the morning.

After seeing his home , his room , parents, every belonging of his made him cry...  He left the house on the 10th day when prachi was kidnapped... And now today he has returned with his love of the life... He thanked God , and all the well wishers...

Rajveer started recovering and gaining his fitness within 3 weeks.... There was a speedy recovery due to his immunity system and also because he was between his family members....

Mrs Rupa and richa looked after him day and night while prachi was looking after her daughter...... Baby hasn't been named yet... Because of the rajveer health issues...

And today is the fourth day ,he went running In the morning to get his speed and health back... He is recovered to an extent....but not fully...

It was 6 am when he returned from running....

Rajveer -Prachiii.... Prachi..... Come here....where are you....

Prachi- I'm here in the balcony, what happened?

Rajveer -I stepped towards the balcony.... I am feeling hot today.... Haven't tasted you for one year almost... Can we bath together?? I told her while steping in the balcony..She was breastfeeding our daughter.... So wholeso me....

Prachi- What the hell!! Why are you here?? Please go ..... I correct my pallu in every possible way.... The balcony has grills and curtains... So I applied curatain all over the grills it is looking like a small cute room.

Im feeling shy.... I know him... His lust... He will start demanding it from me... I have shifted to his room two days before...

Rajveer -Why are you hiding it butterfly...!! Don't you remember I have seen and tasted every inches of yours.... I'll not demand it from you now don't worry ... But I'm not so sure about the night....

Biting one side of my lower lip I'm staring at her.... She became mother and now is feeding my child... I haven't thought of ever that she will do it with her own.... She is definitely a goddess no doubt....

Prachi- What night? Are you insane veer? Disgusting..... ( I don't wanted to use these words but I know him very well, he will do it if he said.... )

Rajveer -What disgusting babe?.... I have right... Isn't it?? Okay so my little fairy has first priority of course... But at least after feeding her you can feed me....

Doctors insisted that I should take a healthy diet and use protein as much as possible.... Breast milk is rich in protein... You don't want me to get healthy as soon as possible??

I know I'm making her uncomfortable by this... But worth it.. her shyness, hesitation to speak, jumbled words... Biting her lips in nervousness.... She is perfect for me.... Her simple, innocent behaviour made me fall for her more....

Prachi- At least break your lust now!! We have baby together.......

Rajveer -So what if we have baby .... The process of making her was more lusty !!

.... I don't have lust, I'm thirsty butterfly!!! ( I love teasing her )

Prachi- Ohh goddd!!! Please!!!! Don't start this in morning.... If you are thirsty go and drink water.... Leave....

Rajveer -Noo... I want your water.... Babe... Let's make it out now... I'll be charge for the whole day.....( I'm just controlling myself trying not to laugh, she is irritated)

Prachi- Veer.... You are so cheap...chii... Why all of sudden you started talking this clumsy??... Are you okay.???

Rajveer -

Yes I'm all okay darling!!! Before i used to talk physically but now it's not going to happen so I'm talking verbally ..... Why?? Don't you like it???

I mean your body don't need it? Touch yourself down there ,I know you are wet .... .. just for me..... And i bite my lower lips seductively....

Prachi- What the hell he is up to..?? Well I'm really wet .... His tshirt and hair is all shaggy in sweat, he has beard which is half trimmed,and the look he's giving ....  fire is heated inside me .... He is Looking so hot, I missed his this look..... I want to feel him ..but not now..... I need inner courage for this... How much he tries to be gentle,but at the end it ends with roughness.....

Okay !! So let's bet..... Will you .??( I said)

Rajveer -Bet?? What bet??? Tell me .....

Prachi- If today you get intimated with me , by any chance I'll be your slave for a week... I mean I will do whatever you say for one week... And if you fail to then you won't touch me with this instance and talk this kinda things ever in life again... ....

Rajveer -I sat beside her left side on the swing... And took my hand on her waist... Started slipping it to her belly....And said in her ears.....

" What do you think of yourself butterfly!??? .... This bet or deal is heavy on me.... It favours you.. it's 99 and 1 . Don't you think?? But ...but... I accept it.... Trust me I will make you habituated of my touch.... In a week itself....

And I leaned to her neck and kissed her shoulder.... Be ready darling.... I'll at home for one month more.... Have taken medical leave....

Prachi- Don't do this.... I said His touch makes current flow through my spine.... I don't want him to know this... And freed my stomach from his hand... Was about to stand up holding baby...He again held my hand...W hat now...???I said

Rajveer -is she done with it? ( Breastfeeding)

Prachi- Yess!!! She is sleeping now.....

Rajveer -I want to taste it... I want to taste what my daughter drinks... Is that sweet or sour or salty??... I want to know...I stood up and hugged her

from back.."Please na.... Just one sip please...I won't force you for more....
Please"

Prachi -Veerr... You are not kid.... How can you even think of it yuck.. it's
so so so so so down market.... How can a person of age 31 ?? Ohh.... How
can a husband drink it... It's nasty...

Rajveer -I tasted everything which was nasty according to you... Like your
cum, you vagina... And..

Please stop..... ( She said)

I never forced you for any kinda thing which gives a men pleasure even
though I forced myself on you.... ( Laugh)

Prachi- Ohhhh! You are irritating me .... Okay fine... But don't bite it....
Just one sip..... You are so stubborn....

I know he won't leave me until he does what he wants ... I'm getting late
for my daily routine.... I agreed.. and went into the room ,he was following
me... Happiness can been seen on his face.... It's really unbelievable how
does he do these things yuck.... No man on this earth does this may be...

I made my daughter sleep in her foster and I myself sat on bed... My blouse
is still open...

He made me laid on bed and removed my saare from my breasts....

Rajveer -You are too beautiful butterfly.... I kissed on her cheeks..

Prachi- I know he's saying this just to make me comfortable, stretch marks
is all over my body.. belly... Thighs...boobs... abdomen... underarm....

The way he's touching my marks... It's like he is admiring it..... I didn't get
a best husband, but he tried and made himself  best husband for me.... I
love him...

Veer I'm so lucky that I got you....

Rajveer -Im lucky that I got you.... You are born for me.... You are divinely beautiful prachi... I love you ... I love you so much.... And I kissed on her lips...

Are you comfortable?....

Yess( she said)

And I shifted down to her boobs...

Prachi- He is caressing my boobs stretch mark with his fingers as if it is precious and rare.... kissing it.... He changed so much.... He's what I have dreamt of....I started breathing heavily ,his touch.... make me high as fuck.... Without doing anything.... To shadow it I said...

Do it fast veer I'm getting late....

He smiled looking into my eyes... It seems like he knows why I tell him to do fast... Godd...

And he took my right bud into his mouth.. ahh... A soft moan came from my mouth... He started sucking it..... While his left hand was holding my cheeks and his right hand was hugging my stomach...

I don't know how to react .. it's giving me pleasure and relief... I kept my right hand on his head and started massaging it.... As if I'm feeding him... My all shyness has vanished...

He didn't bite on it for the first time .. it passed two minutes..... I was so relieved that I forgot to make him stop....

Veer.... Leave me.... Now... It's over.... What will I feed her???.....

He raised his head upon my boobs...

Rajveer -I forgot that it's my angel food.... My fantasies always leads me to problem and regrate..

I'm sorry.... I said her...Please be like this make me sleep....

I'm feeling tired by running.... My body is still not that capable to hold this much... I'm forcing myself to reach my highest immunity..... I kept target to terminate my medical leave within 2 weeks and will join my duty..... Been so many days... I'm feeling bored...

I kept my head on her boobs and hugged her tightly.. .. and tried to sleep...

Prachi- He slept on me... His Legs are in between of mine... Head on my breasts.... I caressed his back and head.... Within 10 minutes he slept.. he's weak now... And doing this much physical activity... No one can make him understand ........ Hufff

He was in his deep sleep I struggle hard to get out of him... He's big to me ... Made him sleep on bed .... And went for shower....

Done Pooja and touched feet of every one... I messaged him to recall our bet... Otherwise he will start making puppy faces to get intimated any time....

I made all my plans to counter him.... Even though it is known very well he will win the bet at last.... But I'll try my best.....

Authors pov- Rajveer is still sleeping because of high doses medicine... Its 10 am ... All are done with breakfast.. rajveer is at last.... Dadi maa is holding their daughter and playing with her..After the breakfast... There was discussion on baby "naamkaran"... (Naming)

All concluded that it will happen tomorrow.... Arrangements were to be made ..... Tomorrow's date was insisted by prachi so that they get busy today and there will be no little hope of him hovering over her.... And at last she will win the bet ....

Rajveer being rajveer.... He made arrangements within two- three hours just on phone call ordering every important things ..... And called clothes seller to the house.... Prachi is shocked seeing his smartness....

Prachi- He's so smart!! How can he win that easy....I sat beside him in the hall on the couch and said..." You are too desperate to have sex... Hmmm"??

Rajveer -Yes I'm.... Im desperate to listen your moans... Butterfly...... I'm desperate to taste you... I'm desperate to take you too heaven.... if it was in my hand I would fuck you here in hall itself.....

Dadi maa-What will you do in hall ? Strangely questioned....

Rajveer -Nooo.... I said in hall there will be decoration for the naamkara n....(Tensed)

Prachi -He's lying.... He said he will do something in hall with me .....

Dadi maa-What will he do?? He's not capable of doing anything right now .... Don't do it... You will be more weak....

She thought of works related to tomorrow's function....

Rajveer -I'm surprised seeing her oversmartness.... She learned how to speak...wahh...good...

Prachi- I was saying same to him... Did you listen  rajveer?  - DON'T DO ANYTHING YOU WILL BECOME MORE WEAK AND WON'T BE ABLE TO RECOVER FAST ..i emphasis on the sentence to tease him....

Rajveer -Yes I understood.... But I'll surely show you who is weak and who is capable of what .... I laughed in devilish tone.....

.........To be continued....Next chapter might

# should I? (+18)

----------------------------------------------------------------

( THANKYOU SO MUCH FOR SUPPORTING YOUR WRITER , FOR LOVING STUBBORN, I STILL CAN'T BELIEVE YOU GUY'S ARE RESPONDING IT... I NEVER EVER THOUGHT O F.... THIS IS MY FIRST STORY.... I KNOW ITS NOT UP TO THE MARK, IM NOT A PERFECT WRITER BUT YOU GUYS ARE SHOWING LOVE IM SO GREATFUL TO YOU ... I LOVE YOU GUYS  THANKYOU SO MUCH.

This chapter got bit longer but will continue.... I have my exams near ... When ever I get time I'll update it.... Your writer is bad at writing you know .... I get lots of struggle in theory part hope you understand.

Thankyou )

At noon 1 pm.

Authors pov- The clothes seller, along with jewellers, were in the hall . All the family members were surrounding them seeing best for themselves.

Rajveer choosed a simple elegant saree for prachi . Rupa taunts him in joke that he has left her and dadi maa while giving priority to prachi.

Prachi brusted into laughter...

Prachi- Papa ji ( Mr Pawan) why don't you gift maa ji one saree... I think she is jealous..... Hahaha....

Mr Pawan -Beta I have given her my whole life and also my blood on daily basis to quench her thirst... I'm not capable of giving her anything.... anymore

(Prachi and all others brusted into laughter)

Mrs rupa- What do you mean by this? Huu?? Im drinking your blood on daily basis... I'll not talk to you.... If I'm that bad than stay away from me ..... ( She said in teasing tone)

Mr Pawan -Prachi, you lead me into difficulty.... Tell what will I do now?? Laughs....

Prachi- Ahhaa!! Don't worry papa ji I'm with you....

(Baby cries she was on the lap of dadi maa)

Dadi maa- Bahu I think she is hungry...... Take her..

Prachi- Ji......

And I took her from the lap of dadi maa... Rajveer is now choosing saree for maa ji and dadi maa... I was never found of jewellery, so they all are choosing it for me.... This family is blessing.... I got one of the best in-laws ..... I'm going in my room now, I also wanted a small nap....First I should feed her.. I sat on the bed and started feeding her........

Hello darling (rajveer)

Ohh shitttt!!! I forgot about the bet..... Ahh!! Why always me!????

Hi darling - I replied

Rajveer -Ahha ! Someone beted with me if I could manage to get intimate with her she gonna obey me for a week.... I just wanted to recall her.....

Prachi- Yeaaa!! I remembered..... No need to.. Go downstairs.... please

My pallu has all covered baby and boobs.... I don't know what is in his head... But I trust him , he won't force himself on me as before....

Rajveer -So you are inside our room... Not you .. we are inside our room... Should I  do it now after you feed her??

Prachi- Nooo!!! Veerr are you kidding?? We will have sex now ? Everybody is selecting gifts... How could you think of it?

Rajveer -What to think about it? One round may be ..??Trust me I'm daying for it.... I haven't felt you since a year....

Prachi- So what? You will do it now..? No way... This is my emergency so I came inside the room otherwise it's not your win okay....

Rajveer -Fine!! So that's it!! If you don't consider it my win than I'll show you my win tonight.... Be ready.... Today your husband is going to punish you.... (Seductive laugh.)

Prachi- For the first time he's using this word and I'm feeling comfortable with it.....

Let's see who punishes whom.!? And it won't be that easy to take me in grap .... I said

Rajveer -And I don't like easy things you know butterfly...... Just I want you to love me the way I love you.... Wait and watch and this will be my first command when I win .... I winked my left eyes gave her a flying kiss and went down.I'm just waiting for night.

Prachi- Huff!! Finally he has gone. I know he is waiting for night but that's not going to be easy "Mr rajveer thakur"....

A sudden plan strikes in my mind... That's full prove he can't even imagine of it.

I patted myself on my shoulder I'm brilliant....Baby cries..........

Ohhoo.... What happened to my little fairy....alelele..... She is feeling slee py...

Let's sleep together your mommy also needs it....  I hugged her from chest and made her sleep with myself...

At the evening.....

Dadi maa-Rajveer, beta go and wake up your wife .... There are lots of things to do for tomorrow rituals.

Rajveer -Ji dadi maa!! I stood up and a sudden thing strikes my mind... She won't come that easy today ...she is definitely planning something... So I just need to close doors...I said -

Dadi maa I'm not going to her....

Dadi maa-Why so??

Rajveer -We have had fight todays noon... And she is hell angry upon me....I'm making plan to calm her down... But I want your help.. would you help me out?

Dadi maa-Ofcourse ill tell me... What can I do?

Rajveer -I am damn sure she won't sleep into our room ... So I want you to force and tell her to get back into room. And I have surprise for her ..... I will make it  out afterwards.... Okay..???

Dadi maa-You are so good in it just like your grandfather.... Okay done!

Rajveer -Done Dana done..... (Both laughs)

Authors pov- When prachi wakes up she saw rajveer is avoiding her, she didn't understood the reason. Meanwhile he was doing this so dadi maa can't caught him lying. Almost all the decorations and arrangements were made, all were done with dinner and prachi was going towards guest room for sleep. That's was her plan to escape from him but rajveer was step ahead.. he called dadi and she made her get into her room. Prachi understood it was him who has done all this ... Not at all surprised she already was knowing he won't lose it.

In the bed room....

When prachi entered into the room rajveer was following her.. baby has slept...

Rajveer -What does my butterfly thought? I will leave her... No chance.

And I grabbed her from waist to Belly.

Prachi- I knew you wouldn't leave me. Current passed through my body... His touch is electric to me...

Rajveer -I love you my Jaan... I told it in her ears.. I want to embarrass her with my love...

Shall we start? If you say yes???

Prachi- He's asking for my permission.... It's weird to give him... For the first time I'll be doing this , I mean before he was forcing himself... raping me...

I removed my belly from his grip and turned towards his face .... Kissed on his cheeks... As a symbol of yes!!

Rajveer -We have baby together but still my wife does not know many things...!! After telling it to her I lined down and bite on her earlobes... . Her hot breath on my chest..... It's so relaxing after a year.... It feels like home .....

I love you .... Prachi .... I love you so much , I can't even imagine my life without you...... I confessed and hugged her tight tears rolled down from my eyes.... God knows how much pain I gave to her.... I'm sorry I'm extremely sorry..... I mermered in myself.

Prachi-

He hugged me tight and I hugged him tighter.... Heard him shobbing..... I raised my head from his chest.... Tears were rolling out on his cheeks.... I wiped them off... I understand his feelings.... In every minute of life whenever he sees me feels guilty....

Rajveer you know what? ..... I said

Rajveer -What ? What does my butterfly want me to know..??

Prachi- I love you.... And ...... I took my both hand and crossed back of his neck.... lifted my foot and started kissing his Crook of the neck.....

He held my waist tightly..... This is so so wholesome....

Rajveer -Babe don't bite it there..... What will I tell to family members..?

Prachi -It's your problem not mine....I said And  bited it... I don't know how do we give marks but I successfully bited it.....

Rajveer -Ouch...! It's not like that.... Wait...i said  And landed my lips on her neck sucking it and bite and then sucking.... It left marks over there....

See babe this is how it is done..... You will kill your husband someday... People will asked what happened...? And the reason is what ?? My wife bited me on neck... ( Laughs)

Prachi- I'm wet.... Just by his kiss on neck...!??? I mermered

Why will I kill you , if you behave this cute everyday I ll be surely dead.... I said .

Rajveer -I can't hold myself more .... I grabbed her lips into mine.... My right hand is on her waist and left on behind of her head...

I started sucking her lips.... Very softly and passionately... I don't want my wildness hover over me... She again locked her mouth with teeth.... I left her lips and brusted into laughter..... Butterfly what are you doing?....I said

Prachi-His lips on mine felt like soft sponge, I was feeling so much good but stopped kissing me..

What am I doing..? What have I done ??.. I said..

Rajveer -Whenever I kiss you open your mouth why you close it with your teeths?I can't taste your mouth.....

Prachi -I don't know....it happens automatically.... Sorry !!I said....

Rajveer -Don't be sorry I holded her cheeks from right side.... See if we kiss open your mouth Don't lock it..... Okay???

She nodded.... Cute like rabbit

Come ... I said.. and she came forward... I held her waist again and head... Started kissing her........ I can feel her breasts up and down to my chest.... Fuckkk I'm hard as rock.... But I don't want it to be fast... Otherwise it will go in rough...

Again she locked it with her teeth.... I won't leave her now.... I spanked her .... Ahhh....she moaned in my mouth and I entered into her mouth....Devouring her .... Testing Every corner of her mouth......

Prachi- My heart is beating fast... different.... I love the way he is gentle while kissing.... I'm losing my breath now!!! We have been kissing from about 10-12 minutes.....

I left his neck... He stopped movement of his lips....

What happened are you okay??... (He said)

Yess... Was just losing my breath... I said...

He kissed me on the forehead and gave me a glass of water to drink after I finished within a minute he lifted me in bridal style and took me to the middle of bed....

He opened his tshirt and than lower... He is nacked just in his boxer... I'm shy as hell....

He hover over me and removed my plates of saree.... A long breathing came out of my mouth.... He smiled.... Im just shy bited my lower lips and turned my head towards my baby in foster....

Rajveer -Look at me butterfly!!... I said and held her chin and made her face towards me ...

I'm all yours..... So why to shy ??? Do we shy by our body also? ..... I said her and kissed on her forehead....

Looking into her eyes I removed her saree from boobs and from her body.... Her boobs were pressed out of her blouse.... My eyes can't get out of it...

I lifted her slightly up and unhooked her blouse.... Slowly opened it and kept it aside... I can't wait to taste her milk.... I put her right bud into my mouth and was to start draining her milk... Until she stopped...

Prachi- Veer!! No wait .....I said, Im losing my control over my body before it takes over me .... I stopped him...." You can't drink it.... It's for our daughter....!! I told him

Rajveer -I know babe its for our baby ...... But today her dad is borrowing some..... I'll not drink it don't worry.... And I started sucking her nipples.... Drops of milk starts coming..... Few drops atleast I can drink.... And I started sucking it more passionately while my right hand opend the knot of her petticoat.

I can smell she is arosen.... I left her nipples I don't want to drink it more just for my little fairy...

I gazed up to see her.... She has closed her eyes and her mouth is slightly open in pleasure.... Fuckkkkk......how much I'm controlling myself god knows.....

I took my face towards her and my right hand has entered into her panty....

Butterfly..... Open your eyes you can't satisfy just by this...... She opened her eyes and met mine..... Perfect and I locked her both hands up of her head from my left hand ..

Look at me..... Don't down your eyes..... She is not uttraing a single word .... Just gazed down.... And my middle finger touches her clit....

I started massaging it in circular...Ahh.....she bites her lower lips and raised her hip.... She is so wet and high....

Do you I it....I asked...

Yessss.....mmmmmm( she moaned)

Should I be more fast..?? I asked in her ears...

Ahhh...yessss......... ( She moaned again')

I started massaging it in anti clock wise roughly......

Ahhhhh.....mmmmmm......yesssss......veerrrre......fuckkkkkk........mmmm mmmm ( she is moaning mess)

What happened butterfly..??? Do you need it...?? ( I asked in teasing tone)

Yesssss .......ahhhhhh......fuckkkkk.....meeeee.....fastttttt( she is raising her hips up and down and moaning)

She is so high ..... Godd..... I inserted my middle finger into her pussy....

Ahhhhhhhh( she moaned)

It's hurting...... Veer..........( She moaned in pleasure and pain)

Yess....it will....because we are having it after an year....( I said)

I waited her to adjust for 1 minute Should I move..... I asked...Yes.....( She replied)

I started thrusting her slowly smoothly from my middle finger...

Ahhh....mmm....ahhh..ahhha...ahhh....yes...... increase it......ahhh.ahhha. hahhh.( she demanded)

I interested my ring finger inside it with middle finger and started thistung her roughly....

Ahhhh.....fuckkkkk.....ahhhh.ahhhha...ahhhh.ahhh.ahh.ahha.hahha.ah.a hhhha.hhhhhh.ahhhhhh.ahhhh.ahhhh.yesssss.....ahhh.ahhhha.hahhh She is moaning like she will fill all the left moan in a year.... Within a 10 minutes she cummed for 5 times....

My dick is hardened as fuck .... It will rip my boxer..... I can't hold it for more now....

Babe are you ready to take me inside.... I said..

Yesssss.....ahhh.ahhhha.hhhh.ahhh.ahhh.ahh.fuck me vveerrrr.....as...hard...as .you...can....ahhhh...... ( She said while moaning my fingers are still giving her pleasure...)

I freed her hand from my grip.. and took out of my finger from her sweet vagina.... It's all covered will her juices.... I licked it.... Every drop of it....

This is nasty? Isn't it my butterfly...? I laughed while taunting her..

She shyed !! After licking it I opened my boxer.... My dick popped out with that and ready to fuck her.

Doesn't you fear this butterfly..?? I asked her in seductive tone...

I do it's really very big for me..... Please be slow and gentle..... ( She said )

I will be don't worry.... Whenever you feel I'm rough tap on my shoulder I'll stop..... Okay..!?? She nodded and I kissed on her forehead.

And went down opened her whole peticoat than her panty.... Fuck its red.. due to fingering....

I want to eat her pussy.... But at first I ll satisfy my little one.....

Touch it ..... And I kept my dick forward to her in between her split legs....

I can't..... ( She said)

Why?? Do you fear ? Trust me!!! for me please touch it.....!!!! I requested her... I want to feel how does my dick response to her touch....

And she closed her eyes and forwarded her left hand towards my dick.... She holded it..... And I holded her hand from up to tighten it.....

Fuckkkkkk.......itsss.....sooo....soooo.... fulfilling..... And it's started to pa in....Thrust me ......give me hand job.... I said....her.....She is struggling to free her hand from it..... I understood she isn't ready now for it......I left her hand...she removed it immediately.....

I'm sorry it's a different feeling.....wired..... She said.

You will be habituated and will feel comfortable don't worry... I said and leaned down kissed on her lips... While rubbing my dick on her clit....

Ahhhhh.....veeerrr..... don't make me wait...... I cantt...... She moaned...

And I get on my knees to thrust her... Inserted my tip inside her...ahhhh. .....she moaned..

And in a thrust I was half inside her..Ahhhhhhhhhhhhhhhhh......hhh hhhhhh.......hhhhhhh...... She started crying in pain... I understand her it's been long ....it will hurt for like first time.... I leaned down towards her face.... And hugged her... Patting her head.... Kissed on her cheeks.... Don't worry wait a bit darling.... it will adjust.... I love you.... I love you so much my butterfly.... I don't want to give you pain.... She is not getting comfortable I decided to pull it out... Im pulling it out.... don't worry.... Please don't cry.... please...I'm sorry.... And I was to pull it out.... Noo....she said while shobing....

I want to feel it... Stop..... Don't.... I Love you too.... She said

Within 5 minutes it adjusted...Move... She said.Are you sure??? I askedY ess..... She said.

And     I     started     thrusting     her     in     slow     pace...
. Ahhhh...ahhhha.hhhha.ah.aha.hahhha.aahhhh.ahhhha...ahhhhha.hhh hhh.ahhhh.ahhhha.hhha.hhh.ahhha ..... She is moaning in pain and ple asure....

Should I slow it down...? I asked...

Noo... She said....

A                         h                    h                    h
.....ahhhha...hahahahha..ahhh.ahhha.hahh...veeeerrrrrr......fuck-
k k k k . . . a h h h . a h h h h a . h h h a . h h h h . a h h h . a h h h h . a h -
hhha.....ahhh.ah.ah.aha.hhh.ahh.ahhha.hahhhhh..... and she cummed for
the second time on my dick.....

It's so fullfilling....

More...... She demanded......

.............

.

...

.

.

To be continued.....

# control (+18)

-------------------------------------------------

Rajveer pov-

After she demanded..... My pace hit harder.... I confirmed are you sure ....???

Yess.....ahhhhhhh.......yes...........(She moaned)

With her moan I inserted my whole length inside her...

Ahhhhhh......veeeeeerrrrrrr......fuckkkkkk....... it hurts........ahhhhhhhhh. .... Her eyes are filled with tears.( She screamed in pain and pleasure)

I can't control myself now..... I locked her both hand and fingers into mine.... And lips into mine lips...

My breath is leaving my body..... I feel so hot inside.... Breathing heavily...... Started sucking her lips and gently biting it.... Ahh...ah.ahh.mmmm.( she moaned into my mouth)

Didn't move inside her for five minutes...she crossed her legs against my torso.... I got it....and started moving .... Slowly....

Mmmmmm......ahhhh.....ahhhhhh.ahhhh.ahhha.hahhhhhamhh..ahhh.a hhh.ahhhh.ahhhh.ahhhh.ahhha.hhhhh.ahhhh.ahhhhh.ahhhh  ( she moaned in pleasure her sound are muffled her lips are cased into mine )

I left her lips to listen her moaning.... I love it from the first day I met her....

A     h     h     h     .     .     .     .     . yesss.....ahhh.ahhh.ahhhhh.ahhhh.ahhhhh.fuckkkk......fuckkkmmmmm mm....yessss....rajveeerrrr.......ahhhh.ahhh.ahhhh.rajjjjjjjjj......mmmmmm mm......youuuu.....aree.......ahhh.ahhhh.ahhhh.ahhhh..bessstttr.........ahh h . a h h . a h . a h . . . . . . . . . . . y e s s s s . . . . . l i k e e e . .........ahhhhhh...ahhhaaaaa.....ahhhh.......thatttttt.....mmmm- m m . . . . y e s s s s s . . . . a h h h . a h h h h - h a h . a h h . a h h . a h h . a h h . . . . y o u . . . a r e e e . . . a h h h . a h h h . a h h h too...gooodddd....ahhh.ahhh.mmmmm...( she is moaning mess)

And she cummed for the 6th time now..Our body colliding sound is echoing with the sound of thrusting and her every moaning takes me higher....

Ahhh....ahhh...yessss.....ahhhhh...ahhhhh..ahhh.ahhh.ahhh..mmmm...yes ss......fuckkkkkkkk......rajjjjj....ahhhhh.ahh.ahhh...veerrrr....ahhh.ahhh.ah h h . a h h h h . a h h h h . a h h h . a h h h h hhhh..mmm....ahahahaha....ahahaha..hhhh.ahh...ahh..yessss....ahhhh.ahh hh.ahhh.ahhh.ahhh..hhh.ahhh...veerrr....mmmmm... ahhh.ahh.She is moaning louder

I locked her lower lip again into mine so that our baby can't be distributed from sleeping....

And started it roughly...was at my verge.... Lust and anger is the thing which I can't control for my entire life .... somehow I managed with my anger issues but this.....fuckkkkk.......Started thrusting her to the core.....

Ahhhh.ahhhh...sloooowwwww......ahhhhahhahhhhh.....slowww...down nnn.....ahhahaha.....veeeeeeerrr.........please......ahhhhhhhh.....ahhhhhhhh.

..ahhhhh.ahhhhamhhh.ahhh.ahhha.hahhhh.ahhhh.... ( she almost cried in pain, I'll regrate as if I wished to be dead .. but fuckkk....myyyyy ......lusttttt....)

Veeerrrrr.....ahhhhaaaaaaaa....... pleaseeee.....ahhhh.ahhhh.ahhhhh.youu u...ah.ah.ah.ah.ah.....ahhhhaaaaa..hhhhh...ahh hurting meee.......raaajjjjv vvveeerrrrrr......ahhh..ahhhaaaaaaaa ............ pleaseeeee.....ahhhhhhhhhh h...hhhhhh

I was about to cum ...... I left her lips....was still thrusting her hard.... Gazed up.... She is all red due to crying..... Whattt ammm....iiiii ..doingggg..???... I can't pull out now..... Why mee... always goddd.... I feel my heart bursti ng.... I decided to pull out... can't give her... pain......

Prachi pov-

I was in heaven,... On clouds.... Best feeling ever in the world...... I wanted him to ruin me.. and demand whole of his length..... The pleasure I was getting is above anything.... I wanted him to be it like for an hour or whole life may be.... But suddenly he increased speed of thrusting.... I was okay with it somehow trying to manage..... And than I got the same feeling when he raped me for the first time.... Same pain ..... Same fear..... I know he didn't do it instantly but it's hurting me like hell.... His dick is touching and thrashing my Womb... I can't hold it anymore..... Brusted into tears.... Scremeing into pain.... Begging him to stop..... Whithin few seconds her left my lips.... He is at his peak I don't want him to feel unsatisfied....but I can't hold him inside me more... It's still very big and painful for me.....

It feels like his dick will rip my pussy apart.... Thrusting in that speed with its whole length.... I choose to let him do until he ejaculate..... He's feeling guilty.... Corner of his eyes are holding tears seeing me in pain.. but his lust.... It didn't forgave me ever till date ...

He was about to pull out.. I said..." Don't leave !!complete it" .... Holding pain inside myself.... My thighs, stomach, vagina is acheing like it will fall down from my body.... Let it be ...... I said to my self trying not to cry lowder and closed my eyes....

He's still inside me... And trusting me...I gave him permission....

" Inside or outside babe".... He said into my ears....

I opened my eyes... And turned my face towards the foster... I don't want to get pregnant again this early.... I thought myself...

And he pulled out cummed on my belly and vagina.... I'm shocked..?? Why did he..? How did he know..??

Looked at his face.... He's biting his lower lip and staring at what he just did ..... I'm feeling shy.... But more than that I don't feel my lower body....in a single round I'm dead..!!!!!

Rajveer -I'm feeling so fulfilling and happy to see her again in my juice.... And sunddly recalled what I have done with her few minutes ago.....

I'm feeling very guilty, wanted to say sorry but how can I?? It's not my first time I have always done this to her .... Always made her cry out of my wil dness.... !!!! Im feeling something is scattering into my chest... Why I can't control myself..??? Why..???  tear droplets ran out of my eyes.....I'm feeling so helpless.... I never knew my lust will take me into this condition.....

I'm angry with myself.... Why do I always do this...???? Whyyyyyyy???????? In every situation I made her cry and now I'm doing the same...... How many swears I have taken I don't know when she wasn't with me but now..... Look at me I'm like an open hungry bull..... I hate myself....I just hate myself........

I wiped my tears... Saw her raising her hand towards me.. I don't want to go near her....my beast will arosen....

Rajveer... Come here....near me... ( She called me)Her eyes are puffed, lips are bited vagina is red , can't move her body just all because of me.....

She called me again.. I strengthen myself and bend towards her hand... ..

Prachi- Rajveer I love you.... I love you so much.... I enjoyed it.... It was the best experience ever I got in my life..... (I said while holding his cheeks to comfort him, and taking him out of guilt)

Rajveer -Don't lie... Please.... I'm sorry.... I always end up in this ..... I'm extremely sorry and  I cried.....

Prachi- Why are you sorry..?? I enjoyed it.... So you don't want me to enjoy???I held my pain inside.. it's okay in love and I comforted him....

Rajveer -Are you sure..! You are lying.... I'm sorry!!! I'm the worst in ever ything....

And kept my head on her chest... Tears rolled down from my eyes to her bare breasts....... Why I'm like this prachi? Why I became monster..??? .... I asked shobbing....

Prachi- Who said you are monster?? ..... You are not.... You are a perfect husband, perfect father, perfect son and a perfect person.... I said him while caressing his head and neck...

I need to change the topic otherwise he'll cry till morning.... My body also needed rest after this....

Veer I want to take bath..... Can I ..??  I said

He up his head and sat near me.. wiped his tears...okay I'll take you to bathroom... Wait.... ( He said)

He wore his nicker and lifted me in his lap and took me towards bathroo m.... Kept me in bathtub....

Opened warmed water and filled the tub added some sopey liquid... And sat beside me .....

I'll make you bath don't worry.... ( He said)

But I don't want him to, i need to release my pain which I have been holding just for him.....

No veer I'll do it myself please.... If I need something I'll let you know...I said

Let me please..... You won't be able to bath yourself to your toes.... Please let me ( rajveer)

No..no I'll if I need you I'll call don't worry.... Please.... Hope you unders tand.... I requested

After that he kissed me on cheeks and left the bathroom....The door closed and my tears started shaading...... It's hurting.... Like someone is digging inside me..... I can't sit in the bathtub.. I can't stand...... What can I do..??

I doesn't find him guilty because he haven't done it knowingly..... He was ashamed of it..... But he has done....I can't change every side of his....I can't..... I laid my head on the corner of tub and closed my eyes.....

Authors pov- It has been a half and hour prachi hasn't called rajveer.... He's tensed but in dilemma she said she will call herself what if he go and she feels bad.... Leaving all this thoughts he opened door of bathroom... He saw her sleeping, head on the edge of bathtub ..... Rajveer rushed towards her... Drained all bathtub water filled with fresh one... Washed her body soap.... She awake.... But didn't tell anything and closed her eyes again in sleep.... After washing her off he took her to bed... massaged her thighs , back , legs........he made her wear night clothes...Baby cries.......rajveer held her in his hand... She was hungry...

Rajveer -Beta your mommy is sleeping.... Come I'll feed you ..... She is continuously crying.... I can't wake prachi she is tired.. but I don't know how to feed a baby!!!!  should call mom??..?? Noo....!!! Hell why am I talking to myself......

Now your dad will make milk for you...for my little princess.... I said her while kissing and Patting her back and chest....

Took her with me into the kitchen.... I should watch videos of how to feed a baby..... I openeed my phone and searched for it within 10 minutes I was done with milk bottle and now it's time to check whether my princess can drink it or not....??

I tasted it on my back palm it was perfect.... And gave the bottle nipples in her mouth.... She started sucking it as if she was starving..... With playing and caressing i took her into room and waited for her to let finish..... She left few drops and was done with it.

Author pov- Rajveer was roaming all inside the room , balcony, swimming pool, with her to comfort her..... Talking with her playing with her..... In few hours she slept again .... Rajveer took her to the foster and made her sleep while he slept after confirming she is fully slept.

In the morning.....Prachi- I'm late today it's 6 am... My clothes are on?... My body is feeling relaxed..... I turned my head he wasn't on bed.... He might have gone for running.... I tried to get down of bed I did it perfect ly.... Pain is almost vanished but have slightly in lower abdomen....

Went to washroom, fresh myself, while taking bath I found his oil fregense in my body..... He might have massaged me last night.... I blushed proudl y.....I changed clothes and done Pooja touched feet of elders.... Ritual will start after few hours.... I have to manage everything.....

Rajveer.....!!!!! What happened.....!!! ???? He came from running and his knees are bleeding with shoulder..............

To be continued......Thankyou for reading stubborn  Hope you are enjoying it .....

# changed

------------------------------------------------------------

Authors pov-After the prachi scremed, all family members Gathered .... Mr Pawan helped rajveer to get him on the couch of the hall....all started questioning him, Worriedly ......

Rajveer -Relax relax relax!!!!! This is not a big deal ..... Calm down.....

Mrs Rupa -What is to relax in this? Tell me how this happened?? You don't have sense where you got injured yourself?

Rajveer -Mommmmm!!!! Why I'll injure myself..?? I suddenly felt dizzy while running and fell down in Rocky areas which led me into this....

Mr Pawan -I was telling you not to push yourself this much!!! Have you ever listened to your elder ones?? And this is your negligence which always leads you to difficulty...... Why don't you understand veer!?????

Rajveer -Dad!! This is not because I'm weak ..!!! But because I was awake all night..... Your granddaughter won't let me sleep..... !!!

Mrs rupa-Where was prachi.!!?? Why don't you tell her to take care for sometime !?? You are not that healthy right now... !! There are no issues to look after her  but you need proper rest for a few more days!!

Rajveer -Mom!! She was tired .... So what happened I did it..?? During my raid duty I used to awake for more than 2 days.... It's okay...!! I'm habituated of it!!!

Authors pov- Rajveer was giving counter excuses to each one in the fa mily....Rupa made prachi understand that he needs proper care now also so she shouldn't ignore his health....Richa and Rishi came..... Rajveer was taken to the room for freshing himself and get ready for rituals..... Prachi followed him... All were in the hall... Prachi's family members also arrived where else rajveer was still struggling for getting himself ready......

Prachi- What are you doing?? Let me help you .... Please..... I have seen everything of yours don't be shy ......I teased him to cool him down.... He was hell angry on everyone after questions answers session that long....

Rajveer -I know you have seen everything, I don't want you to be trau- matized now.... Otherwise I would show you how do we feel shy...... I said from inside the bathroom.....

Prachi- Leave it.... I'm coming.... Its been an hour and he is still struggling with it even though he is not letting me to open his tshirt...?? What kinda behaviour is this ...???? I inned into bathroom..... Hufff.... He's in nicker with tshirt on....

Rajveer -I told you to not come inside.... Why did you...?? If you have came you will have to pay......

Prachi -What pay..??? I have your card take it as much you want it's all basically yours.....

Rajveer -Devilish laugh.... You have to pay by your body..... I forgot that I won the bet.... So from today not now but at night for a week you will be nacked waiting for me to come from jogging and than we will have sex and than bath together.....!!!

Prachi- Whattt???? You have looked at yourself..??? You can't even open your tshirt and last night someone won the bet but at what cost,...??? The cost is he felt dizzy because lack of strength....!!!! I brusted into laughter.....

Rajveer -Is she taunting..???So why don't you check my strength now butterfly?..... I said and kept my lips on hers lip....she is struggling hard to break the kiss.....I won't at any cost now ..!! Until I give her a preview of mine....

Ouch...... She kicked my balls..... Fuck.....ahhaaa......... Shittt.......

Prachi- This was the last option veer.... I'm not going to entertain you now...... I said.

He is holding it and slightly bend towards.... I feel sorry but it is what it is......

Are you okay rajveer??.. I patted his back.... His black tshirt is soked in blood..... I literally forgot about his shoulder..... Goddd.....

Veer...veer...change your tshirt comeon...... I said and started opening it from his back.....

Authors pov- Prachi tried hard to open it , but the tshirt was stick with wounds...... Rajveer was holding his pain and somehow they managed to open it.... Rajveer made prachi out of the bathroom... He know she can't see him in blood....

Prachi rushed to Mr Pawan, her legs are trembling.... Told about the State of wounds.... This was unbelievable that by only falling how can someone get this much wounded?? They come to conclusion that he's hiding som ething....

Dr came and banaged, rajveer... He couldn't wear any full clothes so was just in sando and nicker..... Prachi met her family and was very happy to see them there....

The naming ceremony starts after every ritual was completed it was time to keep baby name.....Mrs Rupa chooses her name as " Priya Raj"Priya from priyadarshini and Raj from rajveer.Every one was happy with it...... Everyone gifted little Priya..... Lunch was done after all rituals and it was time to do something to enjoy full.... music was playing  everyone was dancing solo, couples dance and some were seeing and enjoying it...

Ansh( neighbour)- Bhabi today is very auspicious occasion so will you dance with me..?? If you don't mind...!!!!

He kept his hand forward for her to hold it...

Prachi- Why not!!! Come...!!! I held his hand....And we went to dance floor... Everyone was out there , Richa di - rishi jija ji , his maa and papa, mine maa and papa along with some guests were couple dancing and all others were dancing solo.... Rajveer with ujjwal was sitting on the chair along with dadi maa taking Priya on her lap seeing everyone and talking...

I smiled looking at them and they smiled back...

Ansh-Bhabhi which couple dance!??

Prachi- Is there variety also..?? I don't know... I smiled in delima... I just know basics only...

Ansh-No worries!! We will make it out....

Prachi- Yes ofcourse!!! And he held my right hand in his hand and my waist.... It was not uncomfortable at all..... So I didn't react... He's around 25-26 and a very decent man.... He held me and told me to  keep my left hand on his chest.... It was weird as I never touched anyone till now other than mine husband.... But I kept it.... And we started dancing slowly... With very basic and sweet genuine talks....

After that he left my hands and moved stepped back and pulled towards himself I know this step .... One and only hufff.... Because I was not in high society who would know couple dance.... For every function... After my marriage i didn't get chanced to do so....... Once I have done with reyansh but it was very uncomfortable I was only focusing to get rid of him...

With all these thinking he lifted me up from my waist.... Whattt..!!!!! Noooo!!!! I forgotttt!!! Rajveer...!! He doesn't like this....! How can I ..!?? I was punished two times just because another man touched me one reyansh and one near swimming pool....

I patted on his shoulder he puts me down....

Ansh-What happened bhabhi!?? Are you okay.!?? I'm sorry if I made you uncomfortable.!!!!

Prachi -I looked at rajveer.... He wasn't there...!! I'm tensed.... I replied and want to get out of this now...

Noo..noo... It's time for rajveer medicine... I forgot!! I'll be back don't worry....

Ansh-Ohh thank God!! I thought I made you uncomfortable!!! Please go....

Prachi-And I nodded and went inside the house the dance floor and buffets was organised in backyard...

I ran towards my room.... My heart is beating fast... I don't know how will he react..!! I inned inside the room.... Saw him sitting on the couch eyes closed.... Hand on the head which was hiding his face...

My breath is now living my body...!! Will he rape me again..?? As he used to do before..??? And a tear rolled down from my eyes....I started stepping towards him with trembling legs.... Stopped infront of him...

I'm sorry veer...!! I said in my shaking un clear voice....

He gazed up.... He was crying..... Why.????? ..?????

I wiped his tears in a sec and said...I'm sorry rajveer... I forgot you didn't liked it..!!! I'm sorry please don't force yourself on me please I'm sorry.... And I brusted into tears.... Like he'll do it right now and leave me in pain ....

Rajveer -Why are you sorry..??? I stood up.... And hugged her..... She still has trauma that I'll force myself on her whenever I'll be angry with her ..... I made a big loss in my life..... !!!

I'm sorry for what I have done in past I can't change it na baccha...!!! Im not angry at you just felt bad seeing someone else touching you....! I don't know why but wanted to cry so I came inside room ..... I confessed

Prachi- I smiled... Like I won in my life.... He's fully changed.... If he was old rajveer till this time I would be screaming in pain and begging him to leave me.... I hugged him tighter.... He's jealous..?? May be..?? I'm sorry Rajveer I won't let anyone touch me except you....I said in loving tone..

Rajveer -It's okay..... I said I felt bad!! There is no necessary to force with it.... If you are comfortable you can dance with anyone.... I said

Ahh!! Babe you will take my life.... Your husband is injured you forget.... I know you are arosed and wants to have sex but we can't do it now know!! Everyone might be waiting for us !!! I promise I'll quench your thirst at night..... I said seductively and in teasing tone kissed on her head which was on my chest...

Prachi -

Hufff!!! Why do you always think I am addicted to you..?? God knows who is arosen..... And I separated myself from him ..... .. biting my lower lips...

Rajveer -I'm harden for you...!!! Can you settle it for me..!! ??? ..... Come on let's do it.... And I started stepping towards her..tesing her.........

........

To be continued.....Thankyou for reading stubborn

# obey me (+18)

----------------------------------------------

Rajveer pov-She was taking her steps back.... It looks like daily soaps..... I held her from the waist in a jerk..... Ahhh.. I screamed out of pain,  forgot that I had an injured shoulder..... And left her waist immediately.....

Prachi-Are you okay..??!!! I started caressing his chest...... I'm scared.... In a minute he got normal... Thankfully....

" - don't force yourself and try to act like a smart rajveer.... You are not capable of anything for now take rest otherwise it will harm you"....

He's so stubborn. The doctors told him to rest for at least two months... He started running from the third week.. not only that, he does physical activities too, going to the gym and all.... Nobody on this earth can make him understand

Rajveer -You are right I'm not capable of anything but you are my sweet heart..... So tonight you will fuck me... Let me remind you when I come back you should be in bed without clothes..... Am I clear..????

Prachi-

Are you out of your mind..?? Please!! what kinda Brain you have veer!??

You know it very well I don't know anything about sex and all and you are not in the state of doing it.... I won't do that.... Am I clear. To you???...I said out of irritation

Rajveer -Listen !! butterfly you have to do it at any cost... You have lost the bet... And if you don't know I'll teach you , when will you learn.?? In old age..??

And For your information I won't do anything ,you have to do it.....by chance if you won't.... Don't forget me and my strength.....!!! You have seen so many demos... I smrinked!!!!

Prachi-

Demo..?? Does it mean... Forced..!??? My mind started to flash back... Screaming... Crying.... begging..... My eyes filled with tears....!! Will he force himself on me.?? Noo..nooo... Prachi he can't do that.... He has changed....!!

And I asked him to clarify if he's thinking the same or different...What demo...???

Rajveer -

This morning....!!! Didn't you remember...? Shall we recall it practically.?? ...I said

She was still in the process of what had happened in the morning and I kept my lips on hers..... She didn't resist.... Kept her both palms on my chest.... And I held her waist and neck.... Started kissing her passionately ..... Devouring her mouth.... I can feel her chest up and down due to fast breathing.......

Knock....knock!!! Sudden knock on the door led to break kiss.... We separated ...Rama was at the gate with Priya in her hand....Prachi ran towards her.....

Rama-Choti mam saheb ji she is hungry dadi maa told you to feed her.....

Prachi- Give her to me.... I said and took priya in my hands She was crying, I nodded towards Rama and she left the room....

What happened to my baby..?? She is hungry.!! I started caressing her went to the bed and was about to unhook my blouse..... I saw the left side, rajveer was continuously staring at me.... I felt shy.... He came towards me... And started playing with Priya.... What should I do now?? He won't leave that easy......

" Can you please give me 10 minutes".. I said

He gazed upon me and smiled.... And left the room by locking the door handle....

I unhooked my blouse and started feeding her.... I haven't worn a bra for almost a month or two it is very difficult to open it time and again to feed....

Priya always sleeps in between feeding.... I laid her in bed with me ... Just relaxing my body.....hufff....

Authors pov-

Priya has slept Rama came to look after her while sleeping prachi was needed in between guests........ Every one left after dinner it's almost 9 pm earlier than everyday but they all are tired and need rest..... Rishi and richa left with prachi's family members.... Richa has complications while conceiving so she is on her treatment and one month pregnant.... She couldn't conceive for 6 years in a row when she did, miscarriage happened... But God mercy on her now she is doing well till date......

All the family members went to their bedrooms after settling everything. ..... Priya was awake in between and slept again after feeding....

Prachi pov- I need to take a bath.... There is much hot and I'm sweating extremely.... I confirmed that veer won't come soon in the room before that I'll take a bath and sleep.... I don't want to entertain him today very tired....

Went to the bathroom after checking Priya she is peacefully sleeping in her foster.... Filled bathtub with fresh water and added some fragrance with liquid soap sat in that after u clothing myself.... It is so much relief....

I don't want to get out of this almost 20 minutes have passed.... The door of the bathroom opened.... Fuckkkkkk..... Youuu??....why are you here.??.... Goooooo.... I screamed on rajveer...

Rajveer -

I know your every tactic darling!! You might have thought I'll be late ... You will take a bath and sleep isn't it..?? But unfortunately I'm not!!! .... I said

She is trying to cover herself from a towel which has kept the edge of the bath tub.....she still hesitates...!!! Looking very cute and seductive.... Her hair is all soggy and is spread over her shoulder to back... Water droplets on her body makes divinely beautiful.... She wrapped a towel around her body..... Better for me I can't go in the tub because of injured keen and shoulder.....

Come fast babygirl.... Your daddy is hungry..... I said And I started opening my clothes..

Prachi pov- What the fuck?!!! Babygirl.??? Daddy.??? Yuck!!!! So typical and cheap!!! I'm not your baby girl and you are not my daddy..... Understood that....I said in an aggressive tone...

What happened to him?? He hasn't used such words till date...!! It feels so weird!!

Rajveer -

You are my baby girl and I'm your daddy.... I'll show you how and why!!!Come fast out of the tub otherwise I have to come inside it and you know water is the enemy of wounds...!!! I said

Prachi-

I knew he was in the mood today and won't let me go , he won't force me to have sex but he'll for sure start doing such things which will make me do it ....dhatt...!!!

I'm not scared of having it.... I want him to touch me.... Love me.... Feel me.... But he becomes wild.. he can't control himself.... Which leads me to pain.  He tried hard to control himself but he cannot.... What else can I do?? I have to and came out of the tub...

Now what do you want.??? Let me clear it veer... you get high and rough I can't take this....all of sudden he held me with my waist... Tightened his grip... I am conscious about his wounds on knees so that I can't hit it....

Rajveer -

You are my wife darling and only you have to wear my every single side...!!! I said in her ears and bit on her earlobes.. .. she blushed.....

So I won't do anything today you have to do it !!!... I said and opened the knot of her towel which make her naked but was covered from front because I was holding her waist tightly and my chest was pressing her body....!!

Prachi-

What do you want me to do..?? I won't touch your private parts...!! ..... I cleared!!

Rajveer -Why..?? Are you scared of it...??? Butterfly??? Trust me it will take you to heaven with me..!!! ...I said

Prachi- I don't feel comfortable that's it!!! .... I said

Rajveer -I held her left hand , I was just in a boxer and put her hand inside it..... She hardened her hand to not touch it.... But I insisted on her just once.... And she for the second time touched my dick..... Fuckkkk.....ahhhh I moaned in pleasure.... It's hardened just by her touch.... Babe move your hand in an up and down direction..... I said while closing my eyes it's taking me high!!!

Prachi-

I touched his dick..... He moaned because of me...!???? It was so pleasurable .I have seen him in this condition for the first time.... I am feeling comfortable now seeing him in pleasure.... His dick has become hot and harder..... He told me to move my hands up and down..... I gazed up to see him again... His eyes closed... Mouths are opening and closing while biting the lips of himself.... I made him do that ...!! Feeling proud I don't know why!!!

I took his dick out of the boxer.... I didn't look down just that it will make me panic.... And started doing as he said ..... His cheeks, ears , lip nose along with his neck bone has all turned pinkish red...... His eyes are closed... Biting his lips and moaning my name in between..... He held my hand with a grip I'm sure it will leave marks there......

Babe....ahhhh....fastt.....fastttt......he moaned... Again.... But I can't do it more ..... My hand was losing its grip.... He was on his verge..... I said I can't do it faster veer... My hand is not working now with that speed.....

He opened his eyes.....

Rajveer -

Then give it to me.... And I removed the towel which was in between us.....
I wanted to devour her as hard and rough as possible..... And held her from
the waist tightly ....

Please can you adjust today ...?? I'm losing my control!!! I can't hold myself
for more than long ...... I said... After seeing my condition I know I'll fuck
her till she is finished.....

I'll for sure.... She said and kept her lips into mine.....and I  Started kissing
her, devouring her ,.....

I lifted her right leg and kept on my torso..... And then pushed my dick
inside her without any hint.... She screamed in pain into my mouth..... I
held her waist more tightly with my right hand while my left hand was on
her neck ......

I can feel her warm tears in between our cheeks.... She is removing her leg
from my waist.... I left her neck and held her leg.....

Still devouring her mouth, she wants to break the kiss.... So I left her.......

Veer..... it's hurting me........ You have done it all at once I can't hold it....
Take it out...... She said while shobbing...

I kissed her cheeks.... And said.... Don't worry it will be better...... It will
adjust...... And started kissing her on the neck.... Her hands held my bise
ps..... After a few minutes I felt she turned on.....

Now are you feeling good...??? I asked...

She nodded.... And I started to move inside her...... Ahhhh....veer...... itss s....bigggg.....ahhhhhhhhhhh......... Tears again rolled down from her eyes ..... I stopped moving inside....

Are you okay..??? Should I pull it out?? ... I asked her while wiping her tears...

Noo.. don't...till when you will adjust with it..??.... She said while shobb ing...

I'll be up to when you feel comfortable with it....if you won't feel for a lifetime I won't do it...... I said to her and kissed her forehead....

No need to do this much for me veer.....I always leave you unsatisfied.... I can't even please you... I don't know anything.....I'm sorry  .... She said while shobbing feeling guilty

What do you mean by unsatisfied??? I got the best ever woman in the world... Your single touch pleases me... Take me high .... What do you want more my sweetheart..?? I never ever comply with any of these things.... Don't think so much.... You are perfect just perfect for me my butterfly.... Priya's mommy..... I told her while carrying her hair... She blushed..... And demanded to move....

Are you sure?? Don't force yourself babe.... It's okay.... I said...

No I'm feeling hot inside ,move ..... it's my own decision..... She said...

And I started moving inside her... Slowly..... He left my biseps and held my back.....

Ahhh.........she moaned in the first thrust and started biting my chest.... Nipples..... Sketching my back.... She just turned on.... ..

I              slightly              increased              my              Speed of thrusting....Ahh.ahhha.hhh.ahh......veer....ahhh.ahhh.ahhh............ahh

.ah.ah.ah...........yess....ahh.ahha.hhhh...ahh.ahhh.ahh.....veer.lets go to be d....... Please......ahhh.ahhh.ahhhh....... she said while moaning......

I ignored it and started sucking her collar bones......

Veeerrrrr......ahhhhhha.......fastttttt......ahh.ahhha....yessss......fuckk....mee ...hardddd.......ahhhh.ahh.ahhha.hhhh.ahhhh.ahhhh...hahhh.......yessss...y esssss....more.......ahh.ahhh.ahhhha.hhhhhhh

She started demanding for more...... But I won't give her that easily.... She made me work hard ,she will have to beg for it........ I smirked and pulled out......

She is all shocked and frustrated......

What the hell..?? Why did you do that..?? I want it..... She said and attacked my lips...... Fuckk she is horny today..... I'll eat her raw.... But after I make her yearn for it.....

I separated her from me..... And said... You want it then beg for it baby girl.....tell me give it to me daddy!!.....you have to be my slave tonight what I say you have to do!! After that I'll think about it......

I told her and moved out of the bathroom...

Her face can be seen whole pink in anger and frustration...... I love this.... I'll punish you sweetheart you made me run after you this long.......

.

# Hell-Hevaen (+18)

---

P rachi pov-I want you inside me , but you can't take advantage of this rajveer.... I said in an empty bathroom....

I know now how to do fingering....I'll satisfy it by myself ... And turned on the shower press button of the cold shower... I did it to normalise my willingness of sex .... I parted my legs and inserted my middle finger into my vagina....ahhh...a soft moan has come from my mouth.....

I started moving it .....and then again inserted my ring finger in it.....ahhh h...ouch.....I screamed due to the sweet pain inside it..... This was my first time I did it with myself.

Ahhh.ahhh.ahhhh.ahhhha.....ahhh.ah.ah.ahna.ah.ah.aha.ah.ah whole bathroom was filled with my moans..... I was enjoying it....but rajveer does this better...... Thought of him and cummed......

and the bathroom door has opened..... He's standing there on the door..... Seeing me in shock..... Both my fingers were still inside me..... I didn't pull it out.......

He didn't Uttar a word came near me and turned off the shower Stand before me... He was in his boxer...

Rajveer -

So you are doing my job...!!!! I'll show you how to give pleasure to yourse lf.... I told her... While my face was just 1 inch away from her face....

I'm not mad at her but something is boiling inside me..... I'm feeling overwhelmed.... How can she do it??.... Even if I am here...? Does her ego do it..?? Whatever but for sure I'll take her ability to walk for a week.... I guarantee.....!!!!

I held her hand, can't lift her up due to injured shoulder and took her to room.... Throw her on bed....

That's didn't hurt my feelings or ego whatever!!! But I feel the same anxiety and frustration that I felt years ago..... I'm holding myself... I know I can control it..... I can control my anger..... I can...

" Don't you dare to step on floor otherwise it will the bring the worst..." I told her and moved to drink water which was kept beside the bed on the lamp table.... To make myself calm....

I drank it ... And saw towards her.... Still on bed... Covered herself with bedsheet.... Strangely looking at me.... As if she is questioning what will I do now...!!!!

I went back to her and pulled her from legs towards the edge of bed.... I can't do it in bed hell my knees are also injured.....

Prachi-

I can smell something bad is going to happen again..... His eyes are red.... He's not looking at me!! he's staring at me ... Like want to eat me raw.....

What have I done now.... He left me... I was in need so I did it!!!! But at least... leave it!!.... I wanted it somehow.... What if he becomes wild and doesn't listen to me..????

Nooo!!! That's not possible.....

What are you up to ...?? I asked him in a strange tone knowing what he's up to....

He doesn't respond... What are you doing...??. Ummmm.... He tied the handkerchief on my mouth..... Whyyy.??????? Now he's tiding my hand with his towel keeping it on my stomach... He became completely nacke d.....

Fuckkkkkkk!!! This is not good !!! How will I inform him that he's being harsh on me or not???

And he pushed me on bed and pulled me more towards him by my legs while my upper body was laid on bed and lower part was touching grou nd.....He hovers over me ......

Rajveer -

I took her hand behind her head.... Have tied her hand with my towel and mouth with handkerchief.... And my face towards her... Seeing in her eyes....and said...

" My wife wanted to have sex with me but I denied and offered her to obey me tonight, ..but she chooses to fuck herself own and give pleasure....

So I want to improve my mistake for denying it and will now took her to heaven and than hell, and then heaven again hell, it will go so on hell-hevaen, heaven -hell......

And I took my hand towards her vagina...and started rubbing her clit....She closed her eyes out of pleasure....

Everything which is limited  gives us pleasure!!....and I smrinked while telling it in her ears.... She slightly open her eyes and than closed....

I removed my hand from her vagina... And kept my face on her boobs....
She got it heavy after milking..... I kissed on nipples she breathed long....
And her head rolled back..... She wants me and still chosed to fingering
herself.... Wait wait.... I'll show you ..... And I smrinked after talking with
myself...

I bited on her nipples a muffled moan came from her mouth... And started
sucking it.... Milk drops started coming into my mouth.....And moved my
right hand fingers again into her vagina, instered my middle and ring finger
into it... She moaned and scremed at same time .....

I leftover her boob and shifted to  right boob... Started sucking it, and
moving my fingers inside her.... I started with slow pace.... Her hips are up
and down in pleasure.... I left her boobs alone now...

"Wait butterfly this pleasure will turn into harcore sex pain!!! I said it to
her in a devilish tone.... She looked at me and again closed her eyes into
pleasure.....

Wanted to eat her pussy but can't... I can't sit ..... Why I can't..??? I cannot
sit but she can on my face...!!! ... I said to myself...

And started to thrust her harder with my fingers..... Her muffled moaned
filled room...she is done for now...but I won't leave her.....

Ummmm....veeer.....ahhhhh.ahhhh..ahhhhh.ahhhha.hh.ahh.ahhha.hhh.
ahhh.mmmmmm.ah.ah.ah.ha.ha.ah.ah.ah.ah.aha.ah.ahhhhh.ah.ah.ah.ah.
........ahhhhhhh.ahhhh.ahh.ah........removeeee........ahhhh......ahhh.anbb...
haa...---nnnd.......ahhhhh........ she is moaning I can't hear her all clear...

She's rolling her hips to resist and removed my fingers from her vagina... ..

So I'll leave you now .... Okay .... I said her and took out my fingers all
wet with her cum... I licked every drop of it...still the same as first time...
Fuckkk....

Now it's time for your punishment babe..... I said her and spanked on her pussy... Ahhh... She scremed...

I made her sit by holding her hand and myself laid on bed on my back... She couldn't understand what I'm up to... Held her thighs and made her sit on my chest... She is gazing at me ....I know she won't sit her own.. so I slightly sliding down by lifting her up.. and took my face just on my target..her vagina....

Grabbed her thighs and started licking it... Ahhhh..... She moaned... She didn't resist.... I know she needs me , but till when.????

Started sucking her clitoris... I can feel her hips round and back with pleasure.... Licking every folding of hers.... Ahhhhhh.ahhh.mmmmm.... she's moaning in soft voice .....

I started twisting my tongue inside her and biting it ..... For the few minutes she moaned but now she is resisting.... I tightly grabbed her thighs.... She is displacing herself from my mouth..And started with more roughly... Eating her vagina every folding and clit...Ummm....ahhh...ahhhhh....ahhhhaa..aaaaa......hhhhhhh...ahhha...ah hhh......leave....itttttt.....ahhhhha....pllsseeee......ahhhhaaa...hhhhh.mmm mmm....fuckkkk...ahhhha.......hhhhh......she scremed muf fling .Poor she bend towards bed and held bedsheet for relieving herself of this...

Her muffled moans and scremes are eoching inside room.... My chin ,lips to my neck all is covered with her cum... And with the last bite on her clit I left her... She is totally exhausted.....

I sided her thighs from my grip and laid her one bed  and i stood on  bed .... She is still on the bed.... Holding bedsheet and her face dipped into it....

I turned her around..... She is in progress to be normal...

" It's just a trailer sweetie and you are done?? That's not good!!.. I said her in domanting voice.. and stepped out of bed edge.. pulled her towards myself by her legs...

I want to listen her moans and scremes but it will wake up Priya... So I made my princess wear my sound pad to filter it....

Your mommy is going to be dead my princess, tonight!! I said her and kissed her on forehead... She is peacefully sleeping.....

My butterfly now you can screme out of pain and pleasure as much as you can... I told her and opened the knot of handkerchief from her mouth....

It's over veer I can't do it more leave it for today..... She said while breathing heavily!!

It's not over darling, you have already done what you wanted to do ... now I'll do what I want....!! And I pulled her more towards bed edge and lifted her legs up ....

What are you doing??? Leave me please I'm tired!!!... She said in request..

I have already told you , I'm not going to leave you unsatisfied.... You need me I know... I said and inserted my dick inside her in a single thrust..

Ahhhhhhhh......veeeeeerrrrr.........ahhaaaaaaa.... She scremed... I know it will take few minutes to adjust just waiting for it....

So how can I take this one pain or pleasure... My sweetheart!!??! I promise I'll take you to heaven and then to hell.... Trust me...... You will be addicted to your husbands dick rather than your own fingers...... I told her while kissing her legs .....

Ahhh......just one round..... Not more than that....pl--easee........ Immm.... exhausted..... please...... She said while biting her upper lips .....

Don't worry babe we'll do one round only..... Can I move..?? I asked her if it was comfortable now....

Hmmm......uffff.....move.....she said while closing her eyes.... She still needs me...but her body doesn't allow her... She isn't habituated for this long ....

And I started to move inside her ...... Ahh.ahh.ahhh.ahhh....ahh.ahhh..... ahhh.ahhh..... she started moaing sometimes high sometimes low voice...

And it turns into screaming.... I started thrusting her deep inside .....

Ahhhhhh....ahhhhhh.......doonnttttt.......goooo.......ahhhhhh...... please.........t---ake......itttt.......ahhhhhhhh....outttttt..........ahhhhhhhhhh hhh........and she again cummed on my dick.......

You are asking to take it out while your little pussy needs it more roughly and deeper.......I said her and started thrusting her hard......Her whole body is shaking out of the jerk of thrust...

Ahhhh.ahhhhhh.ahhhhha.ahhhhhh.....ahhhhhhhhhhhh.ahhhhh.ahhhh h...s----lllooooowwww.....ahhhhha...ahhhhhaaaaa..ahhhha.....ahhhhha..... raaaajjjjveeerrr......ahhhhhhhhhhhhhhhh.....slowww...ittttt.....downnnnnn .....ahhhhhhhh.....ahhhhhh.ahhhhhha...ahhhhhha....ahhhhh.......... she is again monaing mess is on her verge but scremeing for slowing it down....... And I slowed it down on her request....... She is herself squeezing her boobs.. biting her lips..... Touching her pussy..... And asking me to leave her?.....drama queen!!!.... And I smiled seeing it how desperately she wants it roughly but demanding for being gentle..... Cute ........

And after it I again started it roughly..... Now no excuses butterfly -I cleared her.....

Ahhhh..ahhhh..mmmmm...ahhh...fuckkkkk......veeerrrr.....ahhhhha...ah hhhh...ahhhhhh..shhhhhhh.ahh.ahh.shh.ahh.ahh.ahhha.ahahahahahha...

..ahhh......myyy....gooooddddddd....ahhhh.ahhhha.hhhhh.ahhhh.ahhhh.ah hhh...... now she can't hide her urge for it.....

I am about to ejaculate so asked her .....Where you want it babee..... Tell your daddy..... !!!

Fillllll...meeee......daddyyyyy.....ahhhhhhhh.......... She said while moanin g...Fuckk!!! Daddy!??? Great..... And I ejaculate inside her........

Can see fullfilling expression on her face..... She loved it...... My dick was still inside her and her legs was still up of my chest.... She closed her eyes maybe she might be feeling sleepy.....

I'm not done yet!! , I told her ,and pulled her by her hand from the bed... She collided with my chest out of the jerk....

" What do you want now ,??please I'm done  I don't want it I can't take it anymore..!!!! She said in a tensed low voice keeping her hand on my bare chest...

But I want it , and this is not for your enjoyment babygirl.!!... This will be your punishment for touching yourself without my permission..... I said it to her while holding her chin and turned her around.....

"Keep your right leg on bed ..... Come on...!! I ordered her...

" Noo, please!!! I won't do it..... Let us end this please rajveer I'm tired...!!! She requested.....

" But I'm not , keep your leg on the bed or else I'll fuck you for whole night.... You know me I can do that..... !! I told her while resting my face on her left shoulder.

She immediately kept her right leg on bed... I grabbed her stomach from back and inserted my dick again inside her.....

Ahhhh...veeerrrr......do it fast..... Free mee..... She said while rolling her head back and landed it on my chest....

I didn't replied to that and asked shall I move..??? Yess.... She replied.... And I started with it with rough........ Her hands are trying to remove my dick from her vagina....

So I warned her ...." Don't you dare it butterfly.... otherwise it will turn into your daily routine"... She immediately removed her hands.....

Ahhhhahhhaaa.....          pl--easee......ahhhhhaaaa.....          leave me.............ahhhaa..ahhhhh.ahhhhhhha.hhhhhha...ahhhhh....ahhhhhhh.. ...raaaajjjjjjjjjj........plllllease.......ahhhhhhh.....ahhaaaaaaaa........ahhhhhhhh hh......iiii.........wontttt.....ahhhhhhhhaaaa.....dooooo......ittt---tttt.....ahhh aaaa......aginnn...ahha..ahha..ah.ah.ah.ah...........sooo---rryyyyy.....ahhhaa... ...... she is screaming and moaning in between...

"I'll leave you soon babe....take it for few minutes more....deep... inside you.... And I parted her legs more and thusted her deep...

Ahhhhhhhhhhhhhhhh......fuckkkkkk.... She screames again.....

And I started thrusting deep inside her... With every thrust her scremes and moaning is getting lowder ....

Nooo.....fuckkkkk......ahhhhhhhaaaaaaa..........itssss......deee...pppppp...ah h  h  h  a  a  a  a  a  a  a  a  .  .  .  .  I  .  .  . can't........ahhhhaaaaaa.....take---eeeeee..........plllleaseeeee.....ahhhhhaaaaaa ....veeerrrrr.......ahhhhhhhhhhhhhh.....ahhhhhhhhhhhhhhhhh......ahha. aaaaaa........ her eyes are filled with tears... I know this was the second time I'm doing it with her in this position, it might be hurting her..... But some sweet pain can be given to her for lessons.

Every corner of the room is filled with her scremes and moans..

I'm not going to leave her that easy, and with my thought Priya Started crying.....!!!!! I got tensed prachi is not in the condition to feed her... What will I do now!??.... Still thrusting deep into her and pulled out my dick.... And told in her ears " Our daughter saved you today".... And I slowly freed her from my grip she was to fall on bed but I held her again in between..... Priya is crying continuously ,I have to feed her....

Prachi is whole exhausted and finsihed..........

# Is megh back?

-------------------------------------------------------------

Authors pov-Prachi was almost going into deep sleep because of weakness. Rajveer placed her on the left side of the bed and wore his clothes , took priya downstairs to make milk for feeding... He successfully fed her as usual Priya slept in between... Rajveer took her to foster and made her sleep there.

Rajveer pov-

Priya is in deep sleep thankfully.... I needed to take a bath and recalled prachi .... She hadn't bathed too... She is sleeping peacefully like a cute baby .... By spiraling her body and her lips pout..... My lust is again knocking the door... ..

I would fulfill it if that wasn't rough before... But my little butterfly can't take it more...!!!my bad!!! Hufff....

I chose to not wake her up for a bath and went to the bathroom , took half a bucket of water with a towel and came to her again...

It's really hard to straighten on her back while sleeping.... Held her hand and tried to make her sleep straight.... Fortunately on the first go she herself slept while keeping her hands on eyes.....

I poured the towel in the bucket and made it dipped into water , squeezed it for removing extra water.... And started cleaning her thighs which are all covered and tightened by my ejaculation...... I really have to work hard for making it clean ...... Three fingers down to her thighs to her vagina is pinkish red because of me......

It's more than a year , but she still get hurted whenever we get into intimacy, we couldn't celebrate our first anniversary, can't even go to honeymoon..... Our life has been shattered in this one year but by the god grace we are together at the last....

I hope we won't face again those kind of situations.... Her body is cleaned now .....

Should I made her wear clothes?? ... Nooo..... Maybe the morning will come with romance...

Now I should take bath....

Authors pov- Rajveer took bath and slept next to prachi after checking out Priya....

In the morning.....(4 am)

Prachi woke up .... Feeling exhausted with body ache..... She tried to sit on bed her hand was pulled backwards and she landed on rajveer s bare chest...

Prachi-

What are you doing..?? I told him in an awkward tone.I'm feeling shy!! My body is nacked, I can feel his chest on my boobs... The sensetion is chilling my spine....

Rajveer -

I'm loving my wife ....!!! Good morning babe..!!! I greeted her and turned myself holding her waist and Hover over her.....

She is nervous...!! I don't know when will she comfortable with it...!! But her this behaviour hits different... Every men out in this world hope for a innocent and soft wife... Of course!! But not in bed , in the life..!!! I automatically smiled seeing her in between sexual tension..!!

Are you okay butterfly.!!?? I asked ..

Prachi-

Yes! Please leave me , I need to go washroom...!! I am very hesitant to tell him this don't know why ..!! But I told.... My uterus will burst now...!!!

Rajveer -

Okay ..! I'll take you .... I told her , she is very awkward telling this .. why????? .... I don't know.... It's normal....!!!

And I leaved her and stood out of bed..

Come..!! I am ready to lift her in my arms... I'm damn sure she won't be able to walk by herself..!!!

Prachi-

No!! I'll go mysleff...!!  I told and  get off the bed ...tried to walk ... My legs are trembling...I'm feeling heavy between my thighs and can't feel my legs.... Vagina is acheing..... Why all of sudden.???

But I tried to walk slowly.... And in a moment rajveer lifted me in his arms.....

Please leave me I'll go ...!! I told him...

Rajveer -

Yes , I can see you can go.....I told her in a teasing tone , And  brought her to washroom..... locked the door.....felt her body is hot...!?? But it may be of the heartbeat when I Hover over her minuets ago...!! What if she has fever.!!??

Okay let her come I'll check it... And I sat on couch waiting for her to come.... It's almost passed half an hour she didn't came.... So I decided to look after her.....

I went to the bathroom... Our bathroom and washroom is attached with a door.... I opened the door of bathroom..... ... Prachiiiiiii......

Authors pov-

As rajveer opened door of bathroom he saw prachi unconscious on the floor...... He got panicked... Lifted her up and rushed towards bed.... Her body is burning in fever...... He tried to make her conscious but it didn't worked out...... He was so panicked that he can't even think what he can do in this situation.... He first dressed her in night clothes... And than rushed towards his mother..... They were all sleeping... He was continuously knocking the door of their room.. Rupa open it and was shocked seeing rajveer panicking maybe for the second time after prachi was kidnapped.... Rajveer told her about the condition of prachi.

Mr and Mrs Pawan came with rajveer  Mr Pawan called the family doctor and both rajveer and Rupa were trying to make her conscious... ... With a water bandage on head ... ..

Doctor came and after seeing her she understood what might be happe ned.... Gave her injection to bring down temperature... And told she has harrasment of work maybe....

And called rajveer out of the room....

Rajveer -

What happened..?? Is she good..? She will be healthy..?? When will be she opening her eyes..?? ... A thousands of questions were running in my mind and I was asking it continuously but stopped when I saw her smiling out of no where....

Doctor -

Beta rajveer!! What should I tell you now !??!!... Im seeing you from chil dhood...!! Look aa.. I mean to say that it happens..!!! When it is done after long time .!!

Rajveer -

What aunty .??? What is done after long time and this happens..?? I'm confused what she is telling...!!

Doctor -

Ummmm...!!! What I'll explain you now....!! It's awkward to tell him , he is like my son.. I have known him since childhood and today is the day when I met him as a husband....!!!

Look it happens when you intercourse after longtime and if that is to passionate and intense.... !! I hope you understand she will be fine in days or two.... ... bye  take care.. and with a long smile I left,  I can't control my smile which was coming from deep down my heart....

He was the same child who was running in nicker, and today he's same.... He has grown up ....

Rajveer -

Ahhh!!! Whattt!????? What she might be thinking..??? Godddd....!!!! She understood everything..??? I'm feeling it's time to underground myself.... !!! Fuckkkk..!! I went inside the room.... Mom and dad was beside her ....

Authors pov-

In around 7 am she got her consciousness back... Rupa was looking after priya.... Rajveer was with prachi.... He was extremely happy when he saw opening her eyes.. he hugged her and kissed her forehead.... After the breakfast she was given medicine.... Her fever has gone in one day and she can't walk normally for 5-6 days and was on her periods which made it worse as much as it could can ... Rajveer pampered her during that with gifts and chocolates making her laugh...... everything he thought he can do .

As rajveer promised her she won't be able to walk for a week......

After a week....

Rajveer was recovered from his wounds, Mr Pawan knew that he was engaged in a fight that day when someone tried to beat him ..... They concluded that it might be people from megh, or any other party who has enimity with him... !!!

He joined his duty back ....... .

In the evening...

Mrs rupa-

Prachi , let's go for shopping today..!!

Prachi-

I'm feeling so shocked, for the first time she asked me about that.... Not because she never wants accompanies me ,!!but she never go for shoppin g......

Yessss... Maaa sure.... What's the reason you are taking me for shopping.. .??? I'm so excited maa ji ... When we will go...???

Anyone can meter my excitement by my face and words...

Rupa-

The reason is I never ever go for shopping after richas marriage, either your papa ji , or rajveer fulfilled my demands or they called sales man into the house....

So I wanted to go with my daughter.... Leave priya with dadi maa and we will  go for it... And back within hour or two.....

Prachi-

Okay maa ji.... I hugged her in excitement... She never ever treated me as daughter in law... When I was brought back from megh ... Everyone was having second thought if he might have  done something with me , but she never ever doubted on me....

When I was new , and taurtered by rajveer I hated him but still that time also I had respect for her..... I love her like my mother.

Authors pov-

Both Rupa and Prachi went for shopping, while Priya was with dadi maa and Mr Pawan .... Rajveer was back from duty but prachi and Rupa were still not at home... .. ...

Mr Pawan called Rupa and she informed that they were in medical shop... Prachi got injuries in her right hand...!!!

He was shocked but choosed not to react because of rajveer he has been very possessive about her after she got kidnapped...... And Mr Pawan told them to come fast !!  didn't asked about what and how this happened....!! Because rajveer was sitting beside him....!!

After an hour prachi and Rupa reached home... Prachis right hand were bandaged.. she was looking all normal...

After seeing her rajveer rushed towards her.... And started questioning uncountable .....

Mrs Rupa told him to not be tensed she is all right ..... They sat on couch...

Rama brought glass of water... Rupa drank it but prachi didn't....

Rajveer -How did this happen..?? Why didn't you informed me.??? How can be you so careless???? .......I wanted to know the reason as fast as I could... My heart has became weak when it comes to her....

Prachi-

I was engaged in a fight and that leads to this....!!

Mr Pawan -

What fight.???? What happened?? Where was driver?? .....

Mrs rupa-

Some of the men's were forcefully making her sit in their car .... The area was empty there were no people... We were going by short cut out of no where 3-4 cars came and two mens opened door and were forcefully making her into the car.... So for protection she used brick which was nearby.... People were gathered after scremeing and they flew away......

Rajveer -

It's strange....!! It's really very strange... !! And I looked at dad.... We conclude with eyes conversation that they might be the same people who attacked on me.... !!

But who are they??..... Non of you will go out until I say... That's final.... Only i and dad will go... Understood...???

And both of them nodded head.

Did it wonded deep?? It pains??? Are you okay prachi..?? And I closed my face towards her hand to see.....

Prachi-

Yes !! It's alright..... What do I tell him?  My fingers and palm have got 5-6 deep cuts ...

I'll change now .... I'm feeling heavy.... !! Where is priya and dadi maa.??? I questioned I haven't seen her yet...

Mr Pawan -

She is with her great grand mother... Enjoying her songs and company... In her room ( Laughs)

Mrs rupa-

I'll be back let me see my grand daughter..... Is she okay or not...!!! Prachi go and change clothes.... I'm there with Priya... Rajveer go with her.... !!!

Rajveer -Yes mom!! Prachi stood up and went to room ....I was following her... How will she open her clothes..? Bath..? Her right hand got injure d..!! I'm tensed... !!

She sat on bed.... Looking exhausted.... I gave her a glass of water to drin k....... Tears rolled down from her eyes out of the blue.....!!

What happened..??? Babe??? Are you okay...??? And I hugged her face to my stomach.... She held my waist from left hand.... She brusted into crying....!!!

I couldn't understand what had happened to her .???

What happen beta.... Tell me... I'm here.... Are you upset..? Tell me please you will take breath out of my body....!!! I told her I can't see her like this.... I'm getting panic attacks again.... I haven't shared it with anyone..... But that's back after 18-19 years..... I asked again what happened babe ??? Won't you tell your rajveer..???

And she left my waist I wiped her tears off..

Prachi-

I'm scared... I'm so scared..... Is megh back.??? Please I don't want to go with him... I can't live without you veer.....I love you.... Save me please..... And I again brusted into tears....

He is my nightmare, the way he treated me .... I can't imagine my life without rajveer... I can't.... My daughter...my family.... What if he's back..?? These thoughts are ripping me into pieces....

Rajveer -

Babe... !!! I held her cheeks and wiped her tears again ... Megh is dead.... Don't you know...??? I have encountered him at that very day.... He's not more....!! Calm down... And no one on this earth can take you from me .... No one... I'm , I was , and I'll always by your side... I love you more my sweetheart.... And I kissed her forehead....

Prachi-

Megh is dead??? I wasn't knowing it... But he can't be dead... You don't know him.... He has always 15-16 doctors ready for him.... I have seen him... He can't be dead veer... He's dengerous..... I know him... He can't be dead...... I said this to rajveer while shobing...

I know megh he can't be dead... It's nearly impossible that his enemy can kill him... He is not that fool... He is alive.... I'm getting bad instincts all of sudden.... I feel someone is watching me.... I felt it from the day I was recovered from my mental instability... But I haven't paid heed to it... His fear... His voices... His face everything is nightmare to me......

Authors pov-

Some one was listening to their conversations............

.

www.ingramcontent.com/pod-product-compliance
Lightning Source LLC
Chambersburg PA
CBHW070344200726
48294CB00003B/778